TROUBLE IN THE STARS

Sarah Prineas

PHILOMEL BOOKS

PHILOMEL BOOKS
An imprint of Penguin Random House LLC, New York

First published in the United States of America by Philomel, an imprint of
Penguin Random House LLC, 2021.

Visit us online at penguinrandomhouse.com

Library of Congress Cataloging-in-Publication Data is available.

Printed in the United States of America

ISBN 9780593204283

1 3 5 7 9 10 8 6 4 2

Edited by Kelsey Murphy.

Design by Monique Sterling.

Text set in Plantin.

Starry sky image by Andrey Pavlov from 123rf.com; Mona Lisa image courtesy of
Wikimedia Commons

To my children,

Maud and Theo,

who are shapeshifters

Across the deepest darkness of space there comes a deeper darkness. It is the biggest ship in the galaxy, and as it moves it is no more than a silent, menacing shadow until it turns and catches the light from a distant sun. The light flickers along its edges, revealing it: huge, bristling with weapons, blotting out the stars.

The ship's name is *Peacemaker.*

Clinging to its belly are small scout ships. Darts, they're called, and each has its own pilot willing to die if ordered to do so. The Dart pilots are highly trained, completely loyal, and they are very young, because none of them tend to survive for very long.

Peacemaker has several purposes, but its main mission is to enforce the laws of the StarLeague. What that means is that it looms over planets that might be having rebellious thoughts, bristles its weapons, sends out a few Darts, maybe fires a warning shot across the planet's polar region, and basically reminds the planet and everyone who lives on it that the StarLeague is the galactic government and rebellion will not be tolerated.

The ship is huge and terrifying.

It is almost the most powerful, most dangerous and deadly force in the galaxy.

Almost. But not quite.

Deep inside the ship, in an ultra-top-secret laboratory, an alarm begins to blare.

There are screams and shouted orders and the sounds of expensive equipment being smashed to pieces. The alarm spreads like a ripple through the ship: *danger*, *danger*, ***danger***, ***DANGER***.

The *Peacemaker*'s bridge—its control center—is a vast room with a gleaming metallic floor; there are ranks of control panels, each staffed by an attentive crewmember. In the middle of the bridge is the command chair, which is currently occupied by General Smag, who is one of the most powerful beings in the galaxy.

One of the most powerful. But not *the* most powerful.

At a control panel, a red warning light begins to blink: *danger, danger, danger*.

At the same moment, a scientist hurries onto the bridge, her footsteps echoing as she races across the metal deck. "Sir!" she pants, and skids to a stop at the command chair.

"Report," snaps General Smag.

"The—the—the—" the scientist gasps. "The weapon—it has escaped!"

And then all is chaos as the general barks out orders, Dart pilots are summoned to their ships, blasters are charged, and the entire purpose of *Peacemaker* shifts. The weapon has escaped. The weapon must be recaptured.

Danger.

Danger.

DANGER.

1

Outer space is dark and empty and silent, and it's really, really big. There are stars, but they are distant and cold. You could drift through space for a long time without meeting up with anything. You could drift for so long that you might forget where you came from and where you are going.

I am a shapeshifter. Currently I am traveling through space in the form of a blob of goo. In this form I'm about the size of a large rat, but without shape or color, like a big, squishy amoeba.

After a long, lonely time floating through the cold, dark, silent nothingness, I detect a space station. When I'm in my blob form I don't have eyes, so I don't see, exactly, but as I get nearer, I can sense that the station is shaped like a huge ring, spinning slowly, brilliantly lit against the darkness.

For someone like me, a space station means danger.

It also means warmth and light and other beings and food.

Don't worry. I don't mean that other beings are my food. I am a shapeshifter, and I am very hungry, but I don't eat people.

Slowly, I drift closer to the station. Closer.

You know what a *pseudopod* is?

Yep, that's right. It's like a fake leg or a fake arm. It's just my goo stretching out so I can hold on to things and pull myself along.

As I drift right up close to the station, I extend a couple of pseudopods and grab on; then I ooze along until I find a hatch—a door leading from outer space to inside the station. Molecule by molecule, I ooze through the crack into an airlock, and from there, inside.

I rest, clinging to a ceiling in a corridor, feeling very hungry. People who live on the station pass below without noticing me. There are insectoids with shiny exoskeletons, and scaly lizardians with big beady eyes, and humanoids with skin that is lavender or brown or peachy pale or tinged with green.

Then along comes a young humanoid with brown skin, pointed ears, and blue hair. Following her is a smaller creature. It is cute and fluffy and has a pink tongue that hangs out of its long snout, and it has a frondy tail. I know this kind of animal—it's a dog. As they walk below me, I sense that the small humanoid reaches out and pats the dog on the head. Then she pulls something from her pocket.

Food. It's a little piece of food. She feeds it to the dog, and the dog's tail wags and wags and wags.

After they pass, I wait until nobody is coming and I drop to the floor of the corridor and shift into a new shape.

Cute, fluffy, four paws, floppy ears, sad eyes.

That's me—a dog puppy.

I practice wagging my tail.

I figure out how to walk with four paws.

I practice making sounds. A whine, a yip, a growl. A bark!

And then I set off to find somebody who will pat me on the head and feed me treats, somebody I can wag my tail at.

I figure I'll have the best luck on the station's docks, a cavernously huge, cold, bright place that is lined with shops and bars and restaurants. It's busy with people from all over the galaxy. The docks are where spaceships come in to pick up passengers and cargo. It's noisy and interesting, and there are giant screens everywhere showing 3D news reports and advertisements, but none of it is colorful, because dog eyes mostly see in black and white. I spend a lot of time going up to people wagging my tail and being adorable and fluffy, but all I get is kicked and shouted at. Everybody is too busy rushing around doing important things; they don't have time for a puppy.

I'm getting better at scrounging for scraps and finding warm places to sleep when something on the docks starts smelling strange—different and slightly wrong. I crouch behind a cargo pod, the deck cold under my belly, and with my keen puppy nose I sniff the air. It smells like danger.

The danger-smell makes me feel prickly all over, and it makes me remember three things that the long, dark cold of space made me forget until just now.

One: I am fleeing from something, but I don't know what.

Two: I am trying to find something, but I don't know what that is either.

Three: I am a shapeshifter . . .

. . . but I am the only one.

2

The space station docks are echoing and deserted, brilliantly lit and colder than ever. Huge barrel-like cargo pods are lined up neatly near each ship's closed hatch, the shops and bars are shut, everything is locked down. The cutest dog puppy on the station has not found anywhere to hide from the danger, whatever it is, and I'm starting to feel a little bit desperate.

Hearing the tramp of heavy footsteps on the cold metal deck, I slink on my belly behind a cargo pod, then peer out to see what's going on.

There's a group of people wearing gray uniforms; on the front of each is a patch with the word *StarLeague* over a picture of a galaxy. Shivering, I watch an officer in their midst who seems more important than the others. He is a tall, broad humanoid, with a heavy chin and a bulging forehead, and in addition to his patch he's wearing a shiny pin at his collar.

Something about him makes me tuck my tail between my hind legs and want to run away and hide.

The big StarLeague officer is giving orders to search the station, something about a hunt for an *escaped prisoner*.

"The prisoner," he says in a deep, booming voice, "escaped from a class-four military prison. It is devious, ruthless, and extremely dangerous. We have good reason to believe that it is somewhere on this space station."

I don't linger to hear any more. Staying in the shadows, I sneak away, then slither through a narrow passage between two shops, where I rest, panting.

My stomach growls, hungry. I growl back at it.

What I'll do, I figure, is stay hidden until the StarLeague soldiers catch their devious, dangerous prisoner, and then I can go on with *my* hunt for a person who will be nice to a cute puppy. Feeling safe in a shadowy alley, I curl into a fluffy ball, and my eyes drop closed.

When I wake up, there is a pair of shiny StarLeague shoes standing right in front of my nose.

"Got one!" the soldier yells in a shrill voice. She's an insectoid, and she reaches down with three of her four arms, and before I can squirm away she grabs me by the scruff of my neck and shoves me into a metal cage.

Wait. *What?*

I yelp, but she ignores me, picking up my cage and carrying me along the dock until we get to a place with a bunch more soldiers in gray uniforms milling around, and cages like the one I'm in.

She drops my cage to the metal deck with a clang, and goes off to report in. I crouch in my cage, panting; it's so cold on the docks that my breath comes out in steamy puffs. Shivering, I peer out to see what's going on.

The cage nearest to mine has a rat in it. Stacked on it are three more cages, all also holding rats.

That sounds like a lot of rats, doesn't it? Four rats is nothing. Believe me, there are a *lot* of rats on this space station.

The next cage is a glass box holding a swarm of insects with brown carapaces, and then there's a glass tank with liquid in it that holds a creature that looks like a swirl of fangs and tentacles. In another cage there's a ball of shiny scales that makes a high-pitched crooning noise.

I don't get it. The StarLeague soldiers are hunting for a dangerous escaped prisoner, right? Why did they capture a bunch of other animals, some rats, and *me*?

I've only just caught my breath when there's a ring of heavy footsteps on the metal deck. An inspection. The big scary StarLeague officer is going from one cage to another, examining each creature.

I crouch in my cage, making myself as small as I can. My dog tongue lolls out of my mouth; I pant with fear.

I am a dog puppy, I think. *I am harmless. Pay no attention to me.*

From my cage, I see the officer's feet, encased in shiny black material, coming closer. My dog nose tells me that he smells like something acidic, with the faintest tinge of metal.

"This, General Smag," says the insectoid soldier, pointing at me with an antenna, "is one of the creatures we caught. Just a dog pup."

The important military officer—the general—steps closer, then bends and peers in at me. I cringe away, squeezing myself into a corner of the cage.

"Maybe it's a dog," he says, "and maybe it isn't."

What? What does he mean by *that*?

Between his bulging forehead and his large chin, his nose and mouth seem too small. His eyes, though, are very sharp. They are completely black and shiny, and he does not blink as he examines me. Reflected in them I see a small, frightened, shivering dog, but I'm not sure what his eyes really see. If they see *me*.

"Hmmmm," his deep voice rumbles. Then he straightens abruptly. "Once we've completed the search, we will examine the creatures more closely. In the meantime, continue to monitor for the energy pattern." The general stalks away, trailed by soldiers. He issues more orders, and some of the soldiers hurry off, while others cluster around some sort of computerlike device that has antennae and blinking lights.

I have a bad feeling that to be *examined more closely* by the general will be an extremely unpleasant experience.

I have to escape.

It's not going to be easy.

Nearby, the rats are sitting quietly in their cages. If I know rats, they're plotting something. Beyond them are the soldiers. There are a lot of them, but they're busy and not actually paying attention to the animals in the cages.

Carefully, quietly, I let myself relax into my blob of goo form. It takes only a few moments for me to ooze between the metal slats of my cage. Using my pseudopods, I creep over the floor, and then I pause.

The other creatures who have been captured. I should let them out.

For one thing, it will create confusion, and maybe the soldiers won't notice that the dog puppy is missing.

For another, they deserve a chance to escape too.

Fortunately, the soldiers are all distracted by their computer device, which is making funny beeping noises. Quickly, I ooze from one cage to the next, extending a pseudopod to open each latch. The rats scurry out, the silver-scaled ball unrolls into an armored animal that trundles across the floor, the insects spill out of their tank and disappear into cracks and crevices, and the fang-tentacle creature plops to the floor and slithers away.

Once they're all free, I creep over the metal deck and hide behind a nearby cargo pod.

And that's when one of the soldiers finally looks away from the blinking, beeping device and notices that the cages are all empty.

"Aaaahhhhh!" he shouts.

At the same moment, General Smag returns with more soldiers. Several of them draw their weapons, on high alert. "What is going on?" the general rasps.

Even my fearless blob of goo self trembles at the sound of his harsh voice.

"The cages." The insectoid soldier points with one of her antennae. "We must have left them unlocked."

The general's beady black eyes flicker, surveying the docks, and then he whirls, barking orders. "The creatures have escaped! We must recapture them all immediately!"

I shift back into my dog puppy form and dash into a nearby alley as alarms start to blare, lights flash, and all the screens on the docks play an emergency warning message. My puppy heart pounds with fright, and I race away, turning corners and ducking into the shadows between two shops, where I crouch, panting and shivering.

A moment later, two StarLeague soldiers running past pause, catching sight of me. With their shouts ringing out, I race down another dark alley and scurry out onto the wide metal deck of the docks. The lights blast down; more alarms blare.

General Smag's giant face appears on all of the screens on the docks. He's shouting orders. There's nowhere to hide.

And I still don't understand. The StarLeague is here to hunt for a dangerous escaped prisoner. So why are they chasing *me*?!

I race in the other direction, and my sharp dog ears hear more footsteps coming.

Skidding to a stop, I look for a place to hide—anywhere.

I dash to hide behind the nearest set of cargo pods, but it's the first place they'll look, they've got me, I have nowhere else to run.

Then I see it.

The nearest ship at dock is an old beat-up freighter, here at the station to take on cargo. It is not a military ship, not StarLeague—its closed outer hatch door is scratched and dented, and there's part of a name stenciled on it in flaking paint: **H n gh**. And as I crouch nearby, panting, its hatch door buzzes and then slowly starts to creak open.

I don't hesitate.

Somehow the StarLeague soldiers don't see me as I bolt from my shadowy hiding place, my paws scrabbling on the slick metal deck. Panting, I race up the ramp, through the open hatchway, and into the ship.

Safe!

A person has followed me onto the cargo ship, but I don't peek out of my hiding spot behind a tumble of boxes to see who it is.

"Close this blasted hatch!" a woman's voice shouts, and then I see, striding past my hiding place, long legs in trousers with a stripe down each side, tucked into scuffed boots. Behind her, the double hatch doors creak shut again.

"Shkkka, release the grapples and get the pulse engines online," she orders, her harsh voice receding as she gets farther away. "General Smag can protest all he wants, but he can't force us to waste a single nanosecond more at this rat-bit station. And I don't want the StarLeague poking its nose into my ship."

"But, Captain . . ." a shrill insectoid voice begins, and they go through a doorway and I can't hear the rest of their words, not even with my sharp dog ears.

There's an echoing metallic clunk and thunk and the deck shivers under my paws. The ship I'm on has just left the station.

The captain must not have seen me, a dog-shaped streak of shadow as I raced into her beat-up cargo ship.

I think I did it. I escaped.

For just a moment I let myself relax, taking a deep breath and resting my nose on my paws. My eyes drop shut. So tired.

My stomach growls, reminding me that I have a problem.

Here's something you probably don't know about the one and only shapeshifter in the galaxy. It takes an enormous amount of energy for me to shift from one shape to another. I have to eat a lot, often. And because of the StarLeague soldiers chasing me, and then capturing me, and then me escaping, I haven't eaten in far too long.

My stomach growls again, louder. *I know, I know*, I tell it, and sniff. The dog nose always knows where the nearest food can be found.

The air smells of humanoid sweat and mold and some sort of spice, and of machine oils, and yes, there is a thread of deliciousness in there too. I get to my paws and trot down the corridor, following the smell of food.

You know this about spaceships, right? The outer doors leading to space or to a station dock are *hatches*, and the doors on the inside are just *doors*, and the floor is a *deck*, and the control center, where the captain gives her orders, is called the *bridge*. And the place where the food is served and eaten is called the *mess*.

Crouching in the doorway, I peer in. This mess-room really is a mess. Along one wall is a galley of sorts—that's the kitchen—separated by a counter from a long table with chairs around it, each made for a different kind of being to sit in. Everything is shabby and patched and grubby, and there's a chunk of half-assembled machinery sitting in a pool of oil on the table, and as I pad across the room, following my nose, the floor is sticky under my paws. The counter is piled with dirty dishes and—my nose twitches—somebody has left a half-eaten sandwich on the table.

In one bound I'm on a chair, opening my jaws to snap up the food, when a big clawed hand grabs me by the scruff of the neck and hoists me into the air.

I give a surprised yelp, and then find two round, slit-pupiled golden eyes examining me.

Oh, just my luck.

One of the crew of this ship is a lizardian. A cold-blooded species that detests anything cute and fluffy, like my current shape.

"What issss it?" asks a high-pitched insectoid voice from behind the lizardian. The insectoid leans closer. She has four arms and two legs, a shiny black carapace, a pincer mouth, and two long twitching antennae.

"Stowaway," grunts the lizardian. Her voice is deep, her eyes are hooded, she has a sharp yellow-spotted crest at the peak of her head, and her broad face is covered with dark green scales, shading to lighter green on her muscled neck. She's wearing a uniform tunic with the arms ripped off, and two belts crossed over her flat chest, and, my dog nose tells me, she smells faintly of cinnamon.

"Whatcha gon' do with it, Reetha?" the insectoid asks. Her pincer-mouth clicks and clacks, and her antennae twitch with excitement. "Eat it?"

"Space 'er," the lizardian, Reetha, answers. Still holding me, she turns and heads out of the mess-room and into the corridor that leads to—

—and I start to squirm in her grip, realizing what she meant by *Space 'er.*

She's taking me to the outer hatch, where she's going to throw me off the ship, out into space.

4

Most creatures cannot survive unprotected in outer space. For one thing, it's extremely cold out there. Also, there is no air to breathe. But before most beings would freeze to death or suffocate, something worse happens. Take a human, for example. You know humans? Warm-blooded air breather with a soft body? Thrust into outer space, a human's bodily fluids, like saliva, sweat, blood, and tears, boil away. Then the lungs rupture, and so do the eardrums, and then this really awful thing called *ebullism* happens, which results in a messy death in just a few seconds.

But I am not *most beings*. My blob of goo form can survive in deepest space with no ruptures and no ebullism.

Even though I could survive—barely—being put out of the ship, I don't *want* to be spaced. I've been in space before, and there's nothing but *nothing* out there for a long, long time. I like people. I *am* people. Space is endlessly dark and lonely, and I hate it.

My dog puppy throat is making pitiful yipping sounds, and I'm struggling as hard as I can to get away, but the lizardian is relentless. She arrives at the outer hatch and hits a button to open it.

This hatch is what's called an *airlock*. That means it's really two doors with a little room between them. It's a safety thing, so that you can't open a hatch directly onto outer space. If you did, the entire contents of the ship, including the crew, would be sucked into space, and everyone would die.

Please, please, please *don't toss me into the airlock, Reetha,* I think. But she does, then hits the button again, and the inner hatch groans shut. There I am, trapped in the little room between the hatch that leads into the ship and the hatch that opens onto outer space. In about a nanosecond, Reetha is going to hit the button that opens the second hatch and I'll be sucked out of the airlock and into the dark, lonely, empty reaches of space.

I don't have much energy left, but I have enough. Just as her claw hits the button, I shift.

The outer hatch groans open, and as a blob of goo I fling myself to the deck, clinging there as the air from the airlock is sucked into space. The deep freeze rushes in, but the shape I've taken doesn't shiver, and it doesn't suffocate. It's not even afraid. It just waits, holding on to the airlock floor. After a long moment, Reetha, thinking the dog puppy is gone, hits the button and the outer door groans shut, sealing with a hiss. Warmer air begins to flow back into the little room that is the airlock. My goo-blob senses can tell that Reetha and the insectoid are leaving, heading down the corridor toward the mess-room and the galley.

I have barely any energy left, and I can only shift slowly, flowing bit by bit into a new shape, one I have never taken before.

When I'm done, my eyes blink open, then I close them again quickly. Even in the airlock there's too much bright color after the black-blue-white of the dog's vision. I open my eyes again, squinting. It's all I can do to climb to my two bare feet and hit the red button that opens the hatch leading out of the airlock. As I stumble onto the ship, an alarm starts to blare, and I hear footsteps coming from the mess-room.

I take one trembling step toward the captain, who is hurrying toward me, followed by Reetha and the insectoid. My vision goes dark around the edges. My legs wobble, and I can feel myself falling. I am completely out of energy. With a thump, I fall to the deck. If they wanted to, they could pick me up and throw me right out the airlock again, and there would be nothing I could do about it. But I hope they won't.

I am in the shape of a warm-blooded mammal. Soft body, no exoskeleton. Air breather. Hair on the top of my head. Hands, feet, face, a mouth for talking with.

A form they probably won't toss out into space. The same species as their captain.

A human.

5

"He's trouble," a voice says. The captain.

"Space 'em," advises Reetha.

"I'm not going to space him, Reetha," the captain says sharply, "even if he is trouble."

I'm lying on a cold, hard surface, and I don't have nice dog puppy fur anymore to keep me warm. I start to shiver.

"The dog must have been his pet," the captain goes on. "And I want to know how they both managed to get onto my ship."

Peeling my eyes open, I see Reetha and the captain standing, staring down at me. It takes me a moment to remember that with a human mouth, I can talk. "Hello," I croak.

The captain eyes me. "What's your name, boy?" she asks.

My name. What was it she called me just now? Oh yes. "Trouble," I answer.

She snorts, then nudges my ribs with the toe of her boot. "What are you doing on my ship?"

I know the answer to that one. "Shivering," I tell her. "Being hungry."

"Let me be clearer," she says with a glare. "*How* did you get onto my ship?"

I'm too weary and too hungry to answer. My eyes close. My entire human body is shaking now, so I curl around myself, trying to get warm.

The captain makes an exasperated noise. "I have to get to the bridge; I don't have time to deal with this. Find him some clothes and something to eat, but don't let him loose to wander the ship." The captain turns on her heel and goes out.

Leaving me with Reetha.

She bends, reaching for me, and I find enough energy to squirm away, but I'm not hard to catch. She grabs my arm with a cold-blooded claw and jerks me to my feet, then drags me along the passageway and into the mess-room.

It's just as shabby and grubby as it was before, but my human eyes can see that the worn, patched cushions on the chairs are brightly colored, and there's a long couch with a blue-and-green patterned cover. The walls are painted in swirls of red and purple, except where there's a big screen, which, at the moment, isn't showing anything. Over in the galley there's a mini-garden stuffed with green leafy plants. It all adds up to a room that is surprisingly warm and cheerful.

Reetha drags me over to a chair at the mess table and drops me into it.

"Trouble," she orders. "Stay." Then she crosses to a locker, opens it, and rummages inside.

While she's doing that, the insectoid pokes her head into the room. Seeing me, her antennae twitch.

I must have taken the shape of an insectoid before, because I know that they are very strong, with all of their muscles inside their carapace, their exoskeleton. To their senses, everything is distant and dim. So far, I like my human shape better.

Except that it won't stop shivering.

"It'sssss awake," the insectoid says. She steps closer, then closer still, and peers at me.

"I'm T-Trouble," I tell her, my teeth chattering. "Do you have a name?"

One of her antennae strokes over my face. Most insectoids' eyes aren't very keen, so the antennae help with seeing things. The pincers at her mouth click and clack, and she says, "Yessss." With one of her four arms, she taps her own abdomen. "Shkkka. We are ship'sss engineer."

"We?" I ask.

"Shkkka, Shkkka, and Shkkka," she answers.

"There are three of you?" I ask.

An antenna taps me on the cheek. *Yes*, she means. Some insectoids are like this—a group mind, so that three of them, or more, think of themselves as just one being. And insectoids are always female. They have a few much smaller males, but the females keep them hidden away, protected.

Reetha interrupts, dropping a pile of clothes onto my lap.

I've never worn human clothing before, so I hold up each piece, inspecting it to figure out how to put it on. There's a one-piece garment with four tubes, one for each arm and leg. After wrestling with it for a while, I manage to get it on and fasten it up the front. The sleeves and legs are too long, so with shaking hands I roll them up. There are fleecy tubes—for my feet—and a shabby colorful top that goes on over my head and immediately makes me feel warmer.

By the time I'm done getting dressed, another one of the Shkkka has come into the mess-room and stands watching. I give her a weak wave, but my attention is on Reetha, who has gone to the galley and is heating something that smells so good, it would make my dog puppy self drool.

A moment later she plunks down a bowl of meat, vegetables, and sauce in front of me, along with a spoon. I've seen humanoids eat before. I close my five-fingered hand around the spoon and dig in. Oh, food, beautiful food, how I have missed you.

"Another?" Reetha grunts when I've finished.

"Yes, please," I answer, and another full bowl lands on the table in front of me. Human mouths can taste food better than any other shape I've taken before. It's *wonderful.*

A bit later the captain comes in and flings herself onto the couch, propping her feet on the low table next to it. A tall, long-faced, blue-skinned humanoid ducks in the doorway, but doesn't come farther into the mess-room. A short while later another member of the crew, a humanoid with tusks and a heavy brow ridge, joins them.

I don't look up from my meal. Reetha brings me more. And more again.

"How much has he eaten?" the captain asks. "How many bowls of stew?"

Reetha brings me another bowl. "Six."

They all stare wonderingly at me as I demolish the sixth delicious serving of stew. Then I lick out the bowl and sit back in my chair.

"Done?" the captain asks with an edge in her voice.

"For now," I answer with a happy sigh.

"Good," she says, getting to her feet. "Because I have some questions for you, Trouble, and you are going to answer them."

I'm full of food and wonderfully warm, and I've never been so sleepy in my entire existence. I drag myself away from the table and flop onto the blue-and-green patterned couch. My human eyes drop closed.

Go ahead and ask your questions, Captain. I'll answer them. Later.

6

Strangely, the first thing the captain asks me about is the dog puppy.

But that's after Reetha woke me up and took me to the bathroom—on a ship, it's called the *head*.

As you probably know, all beings have to eliminate waste from their bodies, though they do it in different ways, more or less smelly and messy. After I figured out how the human body does it, Reetha put me into a shower to get clean. I could have stayed in there for a long time because the warm water felt wonderful, but she dragged me out again and stuck me under a dryer.

As it dried me, I managed to get a look at myself in a mirror.

My dog self was female, but my human self is male. My blob of goo self is neuter, and I've had other shades of gender before. Whatever shape I'm in, whatever gender, I'm always me.

This particular me, as reflected in the mirror, is a young, skinny human male with pale skin, hair the same light brown color as my dog fur, and eyes the same as my dog puppy eyes.

While I was putting on my clothes again—much easier the second time—my stomach growled loudly enough for Reetha to hear it.

"Food?" I asked.

She grunted and brought me back to the mess-room, and I sat at the table while she heated some grains and a milky substance in a bowl and gave it to me.

That's where the captain found me and started her questions.

"The dog was your pet?" she asks. She's slouched in a chair, idly turning a fork in her long fingers.

The captain's face is deeply lined, and her short, tightly curled hair is white-gray, which I know indicates age in a human. Her skin is darker than mine, a warm brown color, and her eyes are brown and very sharp and have a fan of wrinkles at each corner.

"The dog," I repeat, and finish the last spoonful of grains. "Is there more?" I ask hopefully.

Without a word, Reetha sets three more bowls of food on the table, then goes to lean against a wall, watching, her green-scaled arms crossed over her chest.

"Thanks," I say gratefully. Always good to be polite when among strangers. I scoop up a bite of the sweetened grains.

The captain makes an impatient noise.

Oh, her question. “The dog,” I say again, slowly. “Was it my pet?”

“That,” the captain grinds out, “is what I want to know.” She is watching me keenly.

Oh, I know this about humanoids and their pets. They feel an emotional attachment. A real human boy would feel sadness about losing his cute, fluffy pet dog puppy, wouldn’t he?

“The dog was not my pet,” I decide, and pull a third bowl of grains toward myself.

The captain raises a skeptical eyebrow. “It just happened to stow away on my ship at the same time that you did?”

“You did leave your outer hatch open,” I point out. Then I try raising one of my eyebrows the way she just did, but I can’t do it, they both go up. It must take practice.

The captain grips the fork as if she might stab me with it, and then stands and tosses it onto the table with a clatter. She makes a circuit of the mess-room, pausing to kick at a pile of dirty clothes that’s been left on the floor, and comes back to the table, where she flings herself into her chair again.

I start on my fourth bowl of food.

“What *are* you?” the captain asks.

I freeze with a spoonful of grains halfway to my mouth. “I’m a young human male,” I tell her. “I am Trouble.”

Her eyes narrow.

Over by the wall, Reetha straightens. She points a claw in my direction. "Criminal," she says in her deep voice. "StarLeague."

The captain goes very still. "Reetha," she says softly, without taking her eyes from me, "you think he's the escaped prisoner who was being hunted on the station?"

Reetha grunts, and I guess it means *yes*.

The captain leans closer, and her voice has gone cold and low. "*Are* you?" she asks. "Is the StarLeague after you?"

"I don't even know what the StarLeague *is*," I tell her.

Her eyes widen. "The StarLeague is the galactic government. Their military enforces the laws, bringing prosperity and peace to all beings."

Reetha snorts.

The captain gives half a shrug. "Depending on what you mean by *peace*." Then she fixes her glare on me again. "So. Are you an escaped prisoner? Is the StarLeague hunting you?"

"*No*," I insist. "I'm not. It's not."

"Then who are you?" she asks. "Where do you come from?"

"I'm nobody," I tell her. "And I don't come from anywhere."

That part of it is the absolute truth.

But the captain doesn't believe me.

7

Technically, the captain tells me, galactic law allows ship captains to toss stowaways out an airlock, no questions asked. Especially suspicious stowaways who may in fact be devious intergalactic escapees from class-four military prison facilities.

But she doesn't have Reetha space me, even though I can't answer her questions.

Instead she puts me to work.

"It's three weeks until we reach our next stop, at Janx Station," she says.

I'm not sure how long a week is, but in case it's a human thing that I should know, I don't ask.

"We'll dump you at Janx. And," she adds, getting to her feet, "if the StarLeague picks you up there, Trouble, it's your problem. Not mine."

Reetha pulls something circular and shiny from her pocket and gives it to the captain.

"In the meantime," the captain says, "you can make yourself useful. Hold out your hand."

Reetha has gone to stand behind me. A heavy claw rests on my shoulder, keeping me in my chair.

As ordered, I hold out my right-side hand. See? Completely harmless.

Without touching me, the captain leans forward and snaps a shiny metal cuff around my wrist. With a satisfied nod, she steps away. "As long as you're wearing that, you won't be able to leave the mess-room. You going to give us any trouble, Trouble?"

The cuff feels cold and heavy around my wrist. "No," I say meekly.

"Put him to work," she orders Reetha, and spins on her heel. But before she leaves the mess-room, she pauses in the doorway and studies me.

And I study her. She's not happy about something. The situation is bothering her more than it should, I think. Humans, it turns out, are way more interesting and strange than I expected they'd be.

A burp escapes from my full stomach, and my eyes go wide. First time *that* has happened.

The captain shakes her head and walks out.

Reetha doesn't give me detailed instructions. She just waves a claw at the mess-room and says one word. "Clean." Then she leaves.

The first thing I do, of course, is discover what happens when I try to go out of the mess-room.

I step into the doorway, and the cuff on my right wrist gives a warning buzz, and as I start to take another step, there's a crackle, and a crashing shock goes through me, and I find myself on my back on the floor in the middle of the mess-room, blinking up at the ceiling. The echoes of the shock shiver through me, little lightnings of fizzing pain that leak slowly out of my fingers and toes.

So that's . . . what happens when I . . . try to leave the mess-room. Now I know. Won't try it again.

I lie there, staring up. There's probably an on-ship word for *ceiling*, but I don't know what it is. I consider the situation I'm in.

With the amount of food that I have ingested, I have plenty of energy. I could easily shift out of this cuff if I wanted to.

Eventually I will have to, if the captain means it about dumping me at the next station.

I think she does mean it.

They have given me food and warm clothes, and they don't currently plan to toss me out an airlock, and I'm not a dangerous intergalactic criminal prisoner. But I am not safe here.

Or anywhere, but especially not here.

8

Shakily, I get to my feet. There's nothing I can do about my situation for three weeks, however long that is. So I'd better obey the captain's orders and get to work.

I start with the galley—the kitchen. It's a narrow space between two counters, so narrow that a large person like Reetha must have to squeeze to fit in here. Above the counters is a row of orange-colored cabinets, all containing food packets that should be organized according to what different species eat instead of all jumbled together. Below the counters are metal machines for storing other foods and, I discover, for cooking them. I find a bin stuffed with protein bars and take one to munch as I explore the rest of the mess-room.

Just off the galley is a head—a bathroom, remember?—and a tiny closet containing cleaning supplies.

I'm not at all surprised to find that the cleaning supplies are unopened and unused, because the entire mess-room is filthy dirty. The floor is sticky, everything in the galley is almost gummy with grease and spilled food. Scattered around are bits and scraps of wire and plastic and all kinds of junk, and dirty cups, dirty clothes, rat droppings, and tools that probably belong in the engine room. The bathroom is self-cleaning, but clearly nobody's bothered to actually push the button to clean it, and let me tell you, reptilians make a *mess* when they're eliminating their bodily wastes.

I'm on my hands and knees scrubbing at a smear of gunk on the galley floor when a member of the crew ducks through the doorway and into the mess-room. Peering around the edge of the galley, I see that it's the tall, thin, blue-skinned humanoid.

When I pop up from behind the counter to say hello, he startles, flailing his arms, stumbling back until he lands on the couch, where he sits, staring at me.

"Sorry," I say, stripping off the safety goggles I was wearing. "I'm Trouble."

"You certainly are," he says in a wavery voice. "I should have expected . . . The captain said . . . Well." He spreads his long six-jointed fingers over his chest, as if to calm himself. Then he climbs to his feet. He's almost twice my height, so tall that the top of his blue-furred head nearly touches the ceiling. His joints bend both forward and back, so he moves in a kind of bobbing way as he lowers himself into a nest-like chair at the table, folding his legs and looking at me expectantly. "Lunch?" he asks.

I don't know what *lunch* is.

He gives a graceful wave of one of his bony hands. "The midday . . . You know . . . Food?"

Oh, he wants me to serve his meal. *Lunch.* An excellent word to know.

I inspect the food packets in the galley cupboard. "Is stew all right?" I ask.

"I think . . . well, perhaps?" he answers.

I clean out a bowl, figure out how to prepare the stew, and when it's ready, I bring it to him.

Then I make a bowl of stew for myself—*lunch!*—and join him at the table, where he tells me that his name is Ambaratryachnxeftryambanartix, Amby for short. Amby tells me that he is not *he* but *they* because their species can choose any one of five genders, and they say that they like to change sometimes. They are the ship's navigator. I ask them what that involves, and they tell me how wonderful it is being a navigator, although it sounds to me like it's mostly staring at numbers and doing complicated calculations. Then I ask them about the rest of the crew. Amby says that Reetha handles security and communications, which seems strange since she barely talks, Shkkka keeps the ship's engines running, and the last crew member, Telly, manages the cargo.

"What sorts of cargo do you carry?" I ask, taking a bite of stew.

"Ah . . ." Amby blinks. "On this ship it's best not to ask that kind of . . . you know . . . that sort of question," they say primly.

"That's all right," I tell them. "I'm very good at not asking questions."

Amby's response to that is to stare at me, blinking.

Then Amby leaves, and I clean for a short while, and more of the crew comes in. This time it's Reetha, along with Telly, the humanoid with the tusks. "Lunch," he barks at me, so I prepare some stew for them, and also for me, and we sit together at the table. I already know that Reetha isn't a conversational person, so I try talking to Telly, but he ignores me, slurps up his stew, leaving all the parts of it that are meat, and goes out. Reetha follows him.

I clean up after them and wait for the next lunch-eater.

This time it's one of the Shkkka. I offer to make her a meal, but she pushes past me, grabs some food packets from the galley, and takes them with her, back to the engineering section of the ship. I make a bowl of stew anyway, and take bites of it while I'm scrubbing grime off the countertop.

Just after that, another member of the crew comes in. It's the captain.

"Lunch?" I ask happily.

"What are you serving?" she asks, sounding a little grim.

"There's stew," I tell her. "And also stew. I haven't figured out how to make anything else."

She shrugs, so I make a bowl of stew for each of us and join her at the table, setting down a pile of protein bars at my place.

"I tried to go out of the mess-room," I tell her.

"Hah," she says, and takes a bite of her lunch. "How did that go?"

"Could have been worse," I say.

She snorts and reaches across the table to take one of the protein bars at my place. Without me even thinking about it, my hand shoots out, lightning fast, to stop her, the metal cuff banging against the table. Then I freeze, and she freezes, staring at me.

"Hmmm," she says, and slowly moves her hand away.

We both eat for a while, in silence.

I realize something. "Do you have a name? Besides *Captain*?"

She grunts and gets up from the table. Going to the galley, she tosses her dirty stew bowl into the sink and rummages in a cupboard. "Want some kaff?" she asks.

"What's kaff?" I ask.

She pauses. "Huh. Stimulant beverage, served hot. Nasty stuff."

"Yes, please," I say.

A moment later she brings two steaming mugs to the table, setting one in front of me.

"My given name is Astra," she tells me as she sits down again. "It means 'star.'"

"Star," I repeat, and taste the kaff. My mouth puckers up. It *is* nasty.

She slouches into her chair, wrapping her hands around her mug. "For most beings, the important part of this galaxy is its stars. Bright points in the darkness. Light, warmth, color, planets, other beings. Not me." She takes a sip of her kaff. "I like the space in between the stars."

"I don't," I say.

"Why not?" Captain Astra asks.

"It's lonely," I answer.

"It is," she agrees. She gazes at me over the rim of her mug. After a long moment she says, "It's odd, Trouble, that you've never heard of kaff. Humans drink it all over the galaxy."

All I can think of to say is, "Oh."

Tilting her mug, she finishes off her kaff, making a face at its bitterness. She gets to her feet, then leans on the table, staring down at me. "At the station, that StarLeague officer, General Smag, ordered all of the ship captains to attend a meeting, and told us about the escaped prisoner they were hunting. An extremely dangerous being, he said, and—"

"I'm not the prisoner they were after," I interrupt. "And also, I am not dangerous."

"*And*," the captain goes on, relentless, "devious."

"I'm not devious," I tell her.

She nods. "You don't seem to be. But maybe you're so devious that you seem like you're not devious."

"What?" How does that even make sense?

"Reetha has been a member of my crew for a long time," she

tells me. "She doesn't trust you, Trouble, which means I don't either." She leans closer, and for just a second I see in her eyes that space between the stars. Cold, empty, uncaring. It makes me shiver. "Reetha has never been wrong about something like this." She straightens. "Never."

And then she turns and stalks out of the mess-room.

9

Humans, I've learned, like to divide up time into manageable bits. Seconds, hours, days, weeks. I like this idea a lot because it means they eat on a regular schedule too.

We eat, I mean.

Clearly I am not very good at being a human.

I'm so bad at being a human that the captain thinks I'm sneakily pretending to be something I'm not, which is technically true but not *really* true, because I am still me no matter what shape I'm in.

What I need to do, so that I don't get spaced in the next three weeks, is to become better at being a human.

The next morning, after the crew and I have eaten *breakfast*—another new word that I highly approve of—they leave me alone in the mess-room. They're all muttering to each other as they go out, worried that their long-range sensors have detected a *blip*, whatever that is. While they deal with their blip problem, I take the first step in becoming a better human, which is to figure out my own human body.

Flopping down onto the couch, I take off one of my foot-coverings to examine my toes. They're strange. Stubby not-fingers with no apparent purpose. I wiggle them, and then stand to see what it feels like to walk without using them. Ah, I see. Toes help with balance, with walking on two legs.

Next, ears. Ears are even more strange. Fleshy, whorled protuberances, made for capturing sounds and directing them to the hearing mechanism inside my head. Humanoids put decorations on them too. Telly has a row of gold rings in each of his pointed ears.

Telly, I also discovered, loves leafy growing things. At the breakfast table, he held up his hand and said, "I have a green thumb."

Just so you know, his thumb was not any kind of green color.

He went on to tell me that he is a *vegetarian*, which means he only eats things that are plants. No meat. Weird.

Still, I said to him, "I'm sorry that I made you stew with meat in it for lunch. Next time I'll make you something more vegetably."

"Good," he grunted. Then his ears twitched, and he pointed with his fork at the garden on the counter in the galley. "I like salad," he told me.

". . . salad," I repeated, not understanding.

And then he got to his feet and we went over to the garden and he showed me how the vegetables grow, how you put a tiny magical rock called a *seed* into this stuff called *dirt* and it turns into a leafy green plant with roots that suck nutrients out of the dirt.

Seeds, he told me, are the most valuable thing in the entire galaxy, and I didn't have any trouble believing it.

"Try one," Telly said, and pulled up a plant and held it out to me. "This is lettuce."

I popped it into my mouth and chewed. My teeth crunched on the dirt. It tasted . . . interesting.

"You're not supposed to eat the roots," Telly told me, and he made a huffing noise that sounded like laughing.

While we talked, I noticed that one of the gold rings in Telly's pointed ears had a tiny bell on it that tinkled softly every time he moved his head.

Anyway. Ears.

I go to the center of the mess-room and stand still, to practice listening. There's a faint hum coming from the galley, and a deeper thrum that must be the pulse engines, but otherwise the ship makes hardly any noise at all, even though it's hurtling through space.

I flop down onto the couch again, and pull on my foot-covering.

Another weird thing is the fact that male humans have their reproductive organs on the outside. Who thought *that* was a good idea?

But the strangest are my human eyes. Most beings' tender parts are well protected, but human eyeballs are the most sensitive, delicate sensory organs, covered only by eyelids and lashes. And they're wet!

I lie on the couch for a while and practice raising one eyebrow, like the captain does.

Then I get up and circle the mess-room once, twice, three times.

I am noticing that I don't like having nothing to do.

I could shift into the shape of a small creature and explore the ship . . .

No. Better not.

Then I remember another thing that humans do. They *smile*. It means they bare their teeth and turn their lips up. I haven't quite figured out what the smile means to another human. I think it might be a welcoming gesture, but it doesn't make sense to me. When other species bare their teeth, it's meant to be a threat. Still, I practice smiling, too.

When Captain Astra comes in, I am sprawled on the floor with my feet on the couch, smiling at the ceiling.

Lying there, I turn my head and practice my smile on her. "Hello." I try raising one eyebrow, and both of them go up.

She frowns back at me. "What in all of rat-bit space are you doing, Trouble?" she asks, going to the kitchen. It is too soon for lunch, so I don't bother getting up.

"Having nothing to do," I tell her.

She comes out of the galley, unwrapping a protein bar. "It's remarkably clean in here," she notes.

Yep. Apparently I don't have to sleep very much, even in my human body. I spent most of the night cleaning the mess-room until every bit of it sparkles.

And now I have nothing else to do.

I sit up, and the captain tosses me a protein bar.

Something happens to my face. A smile! I didn't have to try at all, it just happened! "Thank you," I tell her.

She stands there for a moment, frowning down at me, and I remind myself that she doesn't trust me and that she could have me thrown out an airlock if she wanted.

"You're welcome," she says slowly. Then she leaves the mess-room, but I don't even have time to flop onto the floor again before she returns. Crossing the room, she hands me a flat, square item made of white plastic with buttons on it.

"What is it?" I ask.

She crouches next to me. "Trouble," she says with a sigh,

"every human in the galaxy knows what this is. It's a remote." Then she points to the screen that takes up almost all of one wall of the mess-room. "It controls the screen. You can use it to look at galactic broadcasts."

"What's that?" I ask.

"Information that's sent out by the StarLeague on screens all over the galaxy," she says, as if it's obvious. "You can also access all of the art created during the entire history of humans." She pushes another button on the remote, and on the screen words scroll past, and then settle. "Also art created by other species." When she gets to her feet, her knee joints crack. "Ow." She nods. "That should keep you busy for a while."

I don't even hear her leave the mess-room.

10

That night I tear myself away from the screen for long enough to make dinner for the crew and clean up, and then I lie on the floor holding the remote, scrolling through *A Compendium of Human Art: Earth, Second Era*. The previous night the crew all left the mess-room right after dinner. But tonight—all except the captain, who is on the bridge watching the blip—they stay, talking and doing things that are fun.

Amby, the blue-skinned humanoid, settles on the couch near me. "This," they say, "is . . . Well, it is . . ." They wave bony fingers at the mess-room.

"Nice," says Shkkka from the table, where she's working on a piece of machinery from the engineering section and also looking at the art displayed on the screen.

"Clean," Telly says. He and Reetha are sitting at a table

nearby, playing some sort of strategy game. He bares his tusks at me.

I smile back at him.

"It's homey," Amby adds primly, and folds their hands over their middle.

Before dinner, Amby and I had an interesting conversation. They came in early, settled in their nest-chair, and asked where I came from. I told them what I'd told the captain, that I didn't come from anywhere. Then Amby asked if I had any family.

Family.

An interesting concept, but not something I know much about.

"No," I told Amby. "I don't. Do you?"

Then they told me about their home planet, where five of their parental units live, along with seventeen siblings who hatched out of the same birth-pod that they did.

Home planet. I think that's what Amby means when they say *homey*, anyway. A family place. I smile at them, take a bite of protein bar, and scroll to the next picture on the screen.

It's quiet for a while and then, at the game table, Telly gives a delighted shriek. Reetha makes a frustrated growling sound and gets to her feet.

"Telly won," Amby explains, unfolding themself from the couch. "And now it's my . . . Well, I get to." They switch places with Reetha, who lumbers to the couch and sits down.

She's watching me steadily with her round, slit-pupiled,

unblinking golden eyes, but I ignore her, my attention on the screen. It shows me pictures of people from Earth.

You probably haven't heard of Earth, the planet that humans originally came from. I had never heard of it either, and I don't know where it is, exactly. Humans are rare, so I'm guessing Earth is pretty far from the galactic center.

The pictures are *oil paintings*, the screen says. *Portraits.* The colors would be blurred smears of blue gray to my dog eyes, but to my human eyes they are so rich and strange. There's one picture that I keep going back to. It's called *The Lady*.

"Reetha," I ask, pointing at the screen, "is this what humans look like on Earth?"

Reetha snorts. "No." With a clawed hand, she rubs at her crest, then nods at the picture. "Old. Ancient."

Oh. *Earth, Second Era.* It must be a long time ago.

The *Lady* in the picture is a human female dressed in black, with long dark hair. Her face is round and pale, her eyes looking off to the side.

Her mouth is making the strangest smile.

I *think* it's a smile.

I get to my feet and take a step closer to the screen so I

can see her better. Is she happy? Sad? Patient? About to stab somebody with a fork?

I try making the same smile with my face.

I think she's happy.

It makes me realize that there's more to being a good human than just knowing how to inhabit a human body. There are also *emotions*.

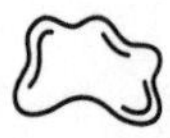

Over the next four days on the ship, I do the following things:

Ask Amby what a *blip* is, and they tell me it's a dot on a screen, which doesn't sound too worrying.

Eat *breakfast*, *lunch*, and *dinner* at least three times each, every *day*, and also this new food called *dessert*.

Learn to play the strategy game and find that I'm so bad at it, even Reetha laughs at me.

Try to remind myself every morning when I wake up that I am not safe here, but it gets harder with every day that passes.

Use the screen to look at all human art from *Earth, Second Era*.

Accidentally shock myself again when I forget about the restraining cuff and try to leave the mess-room with Telly while we are having an argument about the smile on *The Lady*'s face.

Figure out how to make other foods, like spicy rice and beans, slitherbread, and, for Telly, vegetables with soy protein.

And the captain shows me this thing called the *midnight snack*. Neither of us is very good at sleeping, and every night after the rest of the crew has gone to bed, she comes into the galley to talk and make something delicious to eat. Strangely, I look forward to the conversations even more than the food.

You're probably wondering why I like spending time with the person who could throw me off the ship.

Emotions, that's why.

On this night, Captain Astra is at the heating unit making scrambled eggs with cheese powder, and I'm sitting on the counter, asking her what cheese powder tastes like and how it gets that amazingly bright orange color.

"What a question, Trouble," the captain says. "It probably comes from neon cows."

"What's neon?" I ask. "What's a cow?"

The only answer she gives me is a roll of her eyes—an interesting human gesture that I must try.

When we sit at the table to eat, she starts talking about outer space.

"I don't want to talk about space," I tell her.

"Why don't you like it?" she asks, and takes a bite of egg. She makes a face and puts down her fork.

"Because I don't want to *be* spaced," I say, and dig into my eggs. Cheese powder, it turns out, is delicious.

"Fair enough," she says, and pushes her full plate of eggs across the table toward me. "Although at this point I don't think anybody in the crew could be persuaded to toss you out an airlock."

I take a bite. "Devious," I say through a mouthful of eggs, pointing at myself with my fork.

"Uh-huh," she says. "And you have egg on your chin." Hooking a foot around another chair, she drags it closer, then puts her feet up, sprawling in her own chair.

The captain's emotions are interesting to me. And my emotions about her are interesting to me too. When I first came aboard her ship, I was a stowaway and she didn't trust me. And now, for some human-emotion reason, that has changed. Now she makes me feel sort of warm and safe. The more time I spend with her, the stronger this feeling gets.

Is that what human emotions are based on? Time and proximity?

I think it's more than that.

I finish my midnight snack and start on the captain's while she tells me about the deep space between stations. It's always a jolt, she says, coming to a busy, bright, noisy station after being in space for a long time. She loves the feeling of being not-here and not-there, just suspended in the long, velvety darkness. She says that sometimes she sits on the bridge of the ship and listens to the singing of the stars.

"The stars don't sing," I tell her.

"Yes, they do," she tells me, with a strange smile on her face. "You just have to know how to listen."

I don't understand. There's a way of listening so that you can hear things that don't make any sound?

Humans are so weird.

She gets to her feet, yawning. "Good night, kiddo," she says, and then she leans over and rubs my head, ruffling up my hair.

I'm not sure what it means. My dog self liked being patted on the head, and my human self does too.

"Stay out of trouble, Trouble." And she leaves the mess-room.

Talking to Captain Astra about outer space makes me think about being in my blob of goo form traveling through space. The blob of goo doesn't have very much brain or any way of forming memories, and because I spent so much time in that shape, I've forgotten what came before, where I came from.

But I do remember this. When I was out there floating through cold, empty, lonely space, I never sensed anything except silence.

But I do wonder what it sounds like when the stars are singing.

11

I am so, so dumb.

You probably knew this already, but I didn't realize that a *blip* is not just a dot on a screen, it is a *ship* that shows up on the long-range sensors as a dot on a screen.

Yes, the *blip* is a *ship*.

And a ship is something to be very, very worried about.

We're all eating breakfast when the captain stalks into the mess-room. Without speaking, she goes into the kitchen. *Crash* goes a cabinet. *Whack*, she throws something into the recycling tube.

The emotion she is expressing is anger. I swallow a bite of neon-cow cheesy eggs and put down my fork.

“How,” the captain growls, “am I supposed to *make* kaff when I haven’t *had* any kaff yet?”

Another slam of a cupboard, and the captain emerges from the galley carrying a mug. Seeing us all, she stops short, and the hot liquid splashes over her hand. She yelps and then glares at us. “Well,” she says. “I hope you’re all getting a good breakfast, because you won’t have time for lunch.” She wipes her hand on her jacket, drying it. “The blip we’ve been tracking for the past few days is starting to look a lot like a Dart.”

I don’t know what a *Dart* is, but the rest of the crew does, because they all stop what they’re doing and stare at the captain. Shkkka makes a worried hissing sound, and Amby whispers *ohhhh-nooooo*, and Telly barks out one angry word that sounds like a curse.

“Yes,” the captain says grimly, and points at Amby. “Get to navigation and plot evasive maneuvers. We’ll see if it really is following us.”

“Y-yes, Captain.” Amby gets up from the table, bumping it with their knees, and bobs out of the mess-room.

The captain turns to Shkkka. “Did you get the stealth-box fixed?”

Shkkka is already on her feet. “Noooo,” she says with a nervous twitch of her antennae. “Isssss sooo complicated.”

“Well, get to work on it!” the captain shouts, and Shkkka scurries out, followed by Reetha and Telly, heading to their stations.

“See if you can get visual,” Captain Astra calls after Reetha. “I’ll be there in a minute.”

Then it's just the captain and me alone in the mess-room. She takes a drink of kaff and shrugs her shoulders to loosen them. "This has gotten way too complicated," she mutters. I've learned that humans show they are tired by drooping, and they get circles under their eyes. The captain is very tired. Wearily, she sets her mug of kaff on the table and sits down next to me. "Listen, Trouble. I need you to tell me the truth."

"All right," I say, even though I don't really know what she means.

"Are you the reason this Dart is after us?" she asks softly. "Are you being hunted by the StarLeague?"

Her question makes my human body feel shivery and cold. The only thing I can remember is being a dog puppy on the station, and before that, floating through space in my blob of goo form. Nothing else.

Am I being hunted by the StarLeague?

"I don't think so," I tell the captain, my voice shaking.

"Trouble," she says quietly, "you must realize that everyone in the crew likes you, and it's clear that you would like to stay with us. But if you're the reason that Dart ship is following us, we will let them have you."

As she tells me this, I realize that I was starting to feel safe here. What a mistake. It's this human shape. It's making me do stupid things and feel stupid emotions that make me think in stupid, overcomplicated ways.

The captain sighs. "It's evident that you don't understand about the StarLeague."

All I can do is shake my head, a human gesture that means *No, I don't understand.*

"Think about how big the galaxy is," she says. "It's mostly empty space, with stars and stations and planets far, far apart from each other. To keep the people who live in our galaxy ordered, and to keep trade routes running efficiently, the government—the StarLeague—thinks it has to have strict laws, and it has military ships like *Peacemaker* to enforce them. You don't argue with ships like that. If *Peacemaker*'s Dart ship asks to board us, we have to comply. The Dart pilot will check the crew's IDs—your identification chip. You're a stowaway, not a registered member of the crew. If I don't let them have you, they could take my ship and our cargo, throw the crew in prison, and put me on trial. And for other reasons, I can't have them poking around my ship. We don't have any choice about it."

"I don't have any identification," I tell her.

"Everybody has an ID chip, Trouble, even you," she says wearily.

She's wrong about that, though she doesn't know it. Maybe I had an ID chip once, but I've changed shape so many times that somewhere I must have lost it.

The captain sits with her head lowered, not looking at me. "Space is big. People travel with you for a while, and you may like them." She pauses. "Or even love them. But things happen, and you never see them again." She sighs. "That's just how it is, Trouble. You're always alone in the end."

Hearing her say this makes me have a human physical reaction that feels a little like the electric shock I got from the restraining cuff when I tried to leave the mess-room. It doesn't matter if I like the captain, and it doesn't matter if she likes me. Because . . .

You're always alone in the end.

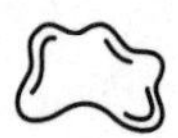

Then the door to the mess-room swishes open. "Captain!" Telly calls, poking his head in. "Report from the bridge. It's a Dart, and it's definitely on our trail."

"*Rats*," Captain Astra curses, getting to her feet and heading out. Then she pauses in the doorway. "You," she orders, pointing at me, "do not leave this room."

I hold up my hand, showing her the restraining cuff around my wrist.

She frowns, nods, and hurries out.

The door closes.

But I'm not staying here.

12

As everyone knows, the most widespread species in the galaxy is the rat.

There are rats on every station, every planet, and every spaceship, including this one. Nobody knows exactly where rats came from, only that they originated at some planet near the galactic center and soon started voyaging out to the very farthest reaches of the galaxy. On the mess-room screen I watched a report about how rats have even reached Earth, the humans' home planet.

Something that not a lot of people know is that rats are very, very smart, and also tricky. At one point in ancient human history, rats attacked using their usual weapon, a thing called *plague*, and nearly took over Earth for their own.

What this means is that the rat is the perfect shape for sneaking and spying.

I shift, leaving my human clothes and the restraining cuff behind in the galley. Feeling extra sneaky-clever in my rat form, I sniff out the trail markers that other rats have left in the mess-room. Following them, I scurry through the nearest rat-hole and then through the twists and turns of the ventilation tubes until I reach the bridge—the command center of the ship. The tube's opening is near the ceiling, so I crouch up there and have a view of the entire room.

The bridge contains a navigation area, where Amby sits surrounded by scrolling numbers and glowing charts, Reetha's communications and sensors area, Telly's area with a cargo computer, and in the center sits the captain's chair, which is shabby and looks comfortable and has stuffing leaking out of it in two places. Next to the captain's chair is a small control panel with a white plastic remote sitting on it and also an abandoned cup of kaff that has mold growing in it. There's a screen mounted on the wall that shows deepest, darkest space, distant stars, and a small, deadly-looking silver arrow that must be the Dart ship.

Captain Astra leans forward in her chair. "No sign of *Peacemaker*?" she asks.

"No," Reetha answers.

"It must be around here somewhere," the captain mutters. "All right. Let's hear what this rat-bit Dart pilot has to say."

In response, Reetha pushes a button on the communication panel.

"To repeat, this is StarLeague Dart ship number 242556982

demanding inspection of cargo ship 90087132. Per StarLeague laws you must come to a complete halt and prepare to be boarded."

The voice is metallic and flat, like a machine talking.

"Telly," the captain snaps. "Get to engineering and see if Shkkka has the stealth-box ready yet."

Telly jumps to his feet. "Stall them as long as you can," he says, and rushes out.

"Now put me through to the Dart pilot," the captain orders, and Reetha pushes another button.

Before she speaks to the other ship, the captain takes a deep breath. Then she leans back in her chair. "Greetings, Dart ship," she says in a slow drawl. "What was that ID number again?"

The metallic voice answers immediately: *"StarLeague Dart ship number 242556982."*

"Didn't you say 242556983 the first time?" the captain asks slowly.

"*242556982*," the metallic voice responds.

"Nine eight *two*?" the captain repeats. She sounds calm, but her leg is jiggling up and down—and that means she's nervous.

"242556982."

I might be imagining it, but the Dart pilot's mechanical voice is starting to sound annoyed.

"A-a-a-and," the captain says, drawing the word out, "you want to do what now?"

As an answer, a bolt of brilliant light flashes across the view screen and the entire ship shudders, while red lights blink frantically on the control panels. Captain Astra leaps to her feet and rips out a curse word.

"*That was a warning shot,*" the Dart pilot's metal voice says. *"Come to a halt immediately, or the next shot will be aimed at your engineering section."*

"Oh no, oh no, oh no," Amby whispers from the navigator chair. "We're doomed."

"Calm down," the captain mutters, still staring at the screen. "We're not doomed. Yet. Reetha, find out where *Peacemaker* is. *Now!*"

Up in the ventilation tube, my rat-whiskers twitch.

I've been thinking.

I'm not the reason for this Dart ship following us. I'm pretty sure it's not me that *Peacemaker* is hunting.

What I *am* is the only shapeshifter in the galaxy. I know that I can't tell anybody about that, not even this ship's crew. In a way, I've been lying to them all along.

I know what this means for me. I was alone before, and I'll probably be alone again, just like Captain Astra says.

But now, in this moment, the ship is in trouble.

And I can help.

13

As fast as my little rat-feet will go, I scamper through the ventilation tube and then out into a corridor until I reach an airlock; getting inside it, I shift into my blob of goo form. The airlock alarm is going off, but I ignore it. Once the inner hatch door is closed, I use a pseudopod to push the button that opens the outer hatch.

Immediately I'm sucked out into space. For a second I float. Space is the same as it always is: airless, deeply cold, empty. The only light comes from distant stars, which are definitely not singing.

From outside, Captain Astra's ship looks like a scuffed and dented cylinder. Ahead, the Dart ship is a much smaller sleek metal sliver.

I need to hurry, because when I'm in my goo form, I can't

remember things for very long, and I do not want to forget the captain or the ship or its crew.

It turns out that my blob of goo form can move pretty fast when it needs to. I zip through the cold vacuum of space to the Dart ship. I don't think Captain Astra will be able to see me from her ship—I'm small in this shape, and my goo is mostly invisible. It takes me only a moment to sense a way into the Dart ship—through its weapons port, hah!—and I ooze in.

It is cramped and dark inside the Dart. The pilot is in a different part of the ship; I need to find a sensitive area where I can do some damage. I worm my way deeper in. Even for my goo it's a tight squeeze. And then, ahead, I sense a pulsing, vibrating area—the ship's engine. When I reach it, there's a metal grate blocking my way. To get past it, I extend a pseudopod through the grate. Like a long gooey finger, it probes the machinery that keeps this ship alive. My pseudopod pulls a wire, and an alarm goes off. More alarms shriek as I pull a few more wires just to be sure, and push some moving parts out of alignment, and then I creep away from the engine area and out the weapons port into space.

I don't waste any time floating around. Quickly, I zip back over to Captain Astra's ship. After getting inside, I shift into my rat form—I'm starting to get hungry with all of this shifting—and scurry all the way back to my perch in the ventilation tube at the bridge to see what's happening.

The captain, Reetha, Telly, and Amby are standing in the middle of the room, staring at the view screen. It shows the Dart ship adrift and broken, thanks to me. It's venting puffs of air that turn into a glittering spray of ice crystals as they hit the deep cold of space.

Hah. I wonder what the Dart pilot will do about *that*!

As you know, space is really big.

In comparison, people like you and like me are extremely tiny, and there aren't that many of us—not compared to the hugeness that is space.

What this means is that when a ship is in danger, every ship in the area must try to help it.

This isn't even a StarLeague rule. It's a people rule. When other people are in danger in space, you have to try to save them.

So there's a long silence as the crew watches the dying Dart on the screen.

"Come *on*," Captain Astra whispers, as if she's waiting for something.

More silence. More air vents from the Dart.

"Anything?" the captain asks.

"No," Reetha answers, after checking the communications panel.

As I'm watching from up in the ventilation tube, my whiskers twitch. I hope I didn't do *too* much damage to the Dart ship. I hope the pilot is all right.

And then, at last, there is a message from the Dart in the pilot's mechanical voice.

"Cargo ship 90087132, this is Dart ship pilot 2425 . . ."

The transmission is interrupted by static.

"*2425 . . .*" the pilot says again, and then there's a sound like gasping for breath. *"Ship pilot 242556982 calling for . . . for assistance."*

"Finally," Captain Astra says. "Telly, get to the cargo area and prepare to take the Dart on board."

"We'll have to dump some cargo pods to fit it in," he warns.

"I know," she responds, still staring at the disabled Dart ship. "Do it anyway. Hurry."

"Right-o," Telly says with a twitch of his ears, and he races from the bridge.

The captain says something else to Reetha, and I realize that I'd better get back to the mess-room. As fast as I can, I scamper through the ventilation tubes until I pop out into the galley. To get the restraining cuff back onto my wrist, I have to shift into my blob of goo shape and put a pseudopod into the cuff, and then shift into my human shape. Then I find my clothes in the pile where I left them, and put those on.

As I'm getting to my feet behind the counter, Reetha and the captain rush in through one door—and at the same moment Telly comes in through the other door, the one that leads to the cargo area. He's carrying something.

It's a body.

14

"Here," Captain Astra pants, and Telly and Reetha sling the Dart pilot's body onto the couch. The body is wearing a space suit—sleek and black, with tubes trailing from it and a StarLeague patch on one arm. Covering the head is a helmet made out of what looks like black glass.

"Get it off," the captain orders. Telly fumbles with a latch where the helmet meets the suit, and then the captain pushes him aside. "Here, I'll do it," she says impatiently, and with a twist and a pull, the helmet comes off.

They all stand there looking down at the body.

I go over and go on tiptoe to peer over the captain's shoulder.

Huh.

"It's a kid," I say.

The girl lying there on the couch has her eyes closed. Her

skin is palest green, with darker green dots sprinkled over her nose and cheeks. Instead of hair she has long tentacles that flow from the top of her head down to her shoulders. The tentacles are a beautiful dark blue at her scalp shading to lighter blue at their tips.

One of the tentacles twitches.

"Is she alive?" I ask.

"Apparently," the captain says.

I push past her and kneel next to the couch. "Hey, other kid," I say, and I reach out and touch her arm.

"She's not a kid, Trouble," the captain corrects. "She's a Dart pilot."

Then the girl's eyes pop open. They are bright green. And they are angry. "Do. Not. Touch. Me," she growls. She starts to climb off the couch, and I scramble away, and then her head tentacles lose all their color and she tips over and falls onto the floor.

Then Amby hurries into the mess-room carrying a box—a medical kit—and pushes me aside, and they and the captain lift the girl onto the couch again and she lies there like a dead bug while Amby looks her over to see what's wrong with her. Telly rushes off to be sure the Dart ship is safe in the cargo hold.

"Will she be all right?" I ask Captain Astra.

"Probably." She doesn't sound happy about it.

"She's not an enemy, is she?" I ask.

The captain shakes her head. "No." She shrugs. "Well, not exactly. We'd rather not have StarLeague military personnel on this ship, that's for sure."

As far as I know, I'm *not* the escaped prisoner being hunted by General Smag and his *Peacemaker* and his Darts, but I *am* a shapeshifter stowaway and I don't have an ID chip, and I'd rather not have this StarLeague pilot on the ship either.

But still. She *is* a kid. Just like me.

The captain tells me to quit standing around and to make myself useful, so I go into the galley to fix lunch for everybody.

After all of the shifting I've done today, I'm ravenously hungry.

Over by the couch, Amby has the girl awake and sitting up. Her head tentacles have turned blue again; maybe that means she's feeling better. The captain is standing guard with her arms crossed, frowning and asking questions that the girl is refusing to answer.

I'm opening stew packets and dumping them into bowls when Reetha comes up to the counter. I get out a packet of the extremely salty snacks that lizardians like. After putting them into a bowl, I hold it out to her.

She's examining me with her unblinking golden eyes. Then

she leans across, takes the bowl, sets it on the counter, and grabs my hand.

"What?" I ask, trying to pull away.

Her claw grips me more tightly. With her other claw, she taps the restraining cuff. "Wrong. Hand."

Oops. When I shifted from a rat to my goo form and then back into my human shape, I got the cuff on the wrong wrist. Trust Reetha to notice something like that. The captain will too, once she's not distracted by the girl. Just my luck, to be surrounded by highly observant people.

Lizardians are much more difficult to read than humans are, so I'm not sure what Reetha is thinking or what emotion she is feeling. She doesn't say anything—not surprising—but she doesn't let go of my hand, either.

Ummmm. "I'm just going to," I say slowly, "go into the bathroom. If that's all right with you." I need to shift the cuff onto the right hand.

Reetha grunts, and then, with her free claw, she reaches into her pocket and pulls out a metal strip—a key—and inserts it into a slot in the cuff. It drops off my wrist and onto the counter.

Reetha lets me go. "Airlock," she says. "Alarm."

What?

She points at me with a claw. "You. Broke. Dart."

Ohhhhh. Reetha handles communications and sensors. When I left this ship to deal with the Dart, she noticed that the airlock alarm went off and the outer hatch opened. Maybe her sensors detected me out there in space in my blob form.

You know what this means?

Reetha knows that I am a shapeshifter.

She stares at me, and I stare back at her.

What's she going to do?

She reaches for the bowl of salt-snacks and pops one into her mouth. Crunching on it, she continues to stare at me. "Dog?" she asks at last.

"Yes," I admit. I was the dog when I came onto the ship.

She nods, like she's suspected it all along.

Then Captain Astra comes up behind her. "Good," she says, seeing the cuff on the counter. "Go keep an eye on the Dart pilot," she tells Reetha. "I want a word with Trouble."

I go shivery and cold, ready for Reetha to tell the captain everything.

But she doesn't.

Without saying anything, Reetha leaves, and the captain pushes me deeper into the galley. "Listen," she whispers. "This Dart pilot was sent out from *Peacemaker* to hunt down that escaped prisoner. They probably sent out twenty or thirty Darts on the same mission. The pilot won't tell us anything, but we don't have *Peacemaker* anywhere on our scans—it's not anywhere nearby—so we're going to be good StarLeague citizens and drop her off at the next station. In the meantime, we won't tell her that you're a stowaway. As far as she's concerned, you're just a regular member of this crew. For the next two weeks, until we get to the next station, just be normal."

"I can do that," I say.

She huffs out a laugh and tousles my hair. "Just don't give anybody any trouble, Trouble."

15

I'm pretty sure there's no such thing as *normal*.

I mean, *you* are weird, aren't you? Yes, you are, and it's not because you have eyestalks or purple scales or webbed fingers or you're a lizardian or a humanoid or whatever.

Every person is themself, and that makes us all different and weird to each other.

Except for me. I'm a little weirder than everybody else.

In the galley, I make stew for most of us, and lettuce without roots for Telly.

Over on the other side of the mess-room, the girl has stripped down to a black coverall with a StarLeague patch on the front. Her head-tentacles have turned deep blue again, and she's tied them back from her face. In height, she is somewhere between me and the captain, and at a guess she is about the same age that I seem to be, in my human shape. She is thin, but she looks strong. She moves like she's had training. She's probably deadly. *And* devious.

"Let's eat," the captain says, and everybody, including the girl, gathers around the table.

Stew, delicious stew. Cubes of protein and cubes of plant matter swimming in a salty brown sauce. *Mmmmmmm.*

While the girl eats, she watches the rest of us. And we watch her.

I notice that she chews every bite exactly ten times before swallowing. She sits with her spine straight, not touching the back of her chair.

"What's your name?" I ask her.

She sets down her spoon, and it is lined up precisely next to her bowl. "StarLeague pilot 242556982."

"That's not a name," I point out. "It's a number."

She doesn't say anything. One of her blue hair-tentacles escapes from the tie and waves free.

"My name is Trouble," I tell her, and take a bite of stew. "With a T."

The girl reaches up and tucks the free tentacle behind her ear. After another long moment she says, "My name is Electra." Then she looks sharply at me. "Who *are* you, exactly?"

"He's nobody," the captain puts in from the end of the table.

"I doubt that you are *nobody*," Electra says to me.

I blink. "I'm definitely nobody," I tell her.

"He cooks and keeps the galley clean," Captain Astra says. "He won't give you any trouble."

And I would smile at that, because I know she said *trouble* for me, like a shared secret, except that Electra is still watching me.

Finishing my stew, I lick my bowl and put it on the table. I gaze longingly at everybody else's dinners.

Unfortunately, because of all the shapeshifting I've done today, I'm *extremely* hungry. But all I have to do is eat eight bowls of stew in front of Electra for her to realize that I'm not normal.

"More stew?" the captain asks me, getting up and walking into the galley.

"No, thank you," I say.

The entire crew stops eating and stares at me.

My stomach growls, loudly.

"I'm not hungry," I add.

The captain gives me an odd look. When she comes out of the galley, she puts a pile of protein bars next to my empty stew bowl.

I sit on my hands so that I don't reach for a protein bar. Everybody else goes back to their stew. Electra keeps watching me.

Growl, growl, growl goes my stomach.

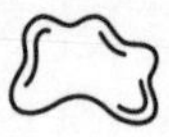

After dinner, the rest of the crew hurries out. Captain Astra wants Reetha to check on whether *Peacemaker* is pursuing us, because maybe Electra sent them a message before her Dart ship became disabled. Shkkka is sent to inspect the Dart and to continue working on the stealth-box, whatever that is, and Amby is supposed to set a course to make it harder for any other ships to follow us.

On the captain's orders, Telly puts the restraining cuff onto Electra. Then he goes out.

Electra does the same thing I did after the captain put the cuff on me.

She heads for the doorway that leads out of the mess-room.

"Don't try it," I tell her, following.

She ignores me and hits the panel to open the door.

"You'll get a terrible"—I start to say, and then she's stepping through, and—"shock," I finish as the restraining cuff crackles and she's flung back into the mess-room.

She's lying on the floor in the middle of the room. I go and crouch next to her. She's staring up at the ceiling without blinking. I pat her on the arm.

She takes a gasping breath.

"It's all right," I tell her. "It'll stop hurting in a few seconds."

She takes another breath, then starts struggling to sit up. I try to help, and she jerks away. "Leave me," she hisses, "alone."

With a shrug, I go to sit with my back against the wall. Slowly, she manages to sit up, leaning against the couch.

"Are you all right?" I ask.

"I am not," she says stiffly, "speaking to you."

We sit in silence for a few minutes.

Electra's voice is low and angry. "But I'll tell you one thing—"

"I thought you weren't speaking to me," I interrupt.

"Shut up," she snaps. "The captain of this tin-can ship is going to be sorry about this." She holds up her hand, showing the cuff around her wrist. Then she climbs shakily to her feet. "I am a StarLeague cadet and a Dart pilot. I was sent on a mission to locate and, if possible, recapture an escaped criminal." She scowls down at me. "My mission hasn't ended just because my Dart was damaged. If there's something not right about this ship and its crew, I *will* find out."

16

I should probably tell you more about the ship that we're on.

During one of our long, interesting midnight snack conversations, the captain told me that the ship is named *Hindsight.*

"What does that mean?" I asked her.

She gave half a laugh. "*Hindsight* means understanding something only after it's happened, and not while it's happening. It means knowing better next time."

I hope there is a next time, so I can know better about it.

Anyway, I figure that if I'm not wearing the restraining cuff anymore, I can go anywhere on the *Hindsight* that I want to. Exploring, I find out that at one end of the ship are the living areas—the mess-room and tiny sleeping rooms for each of the crew—in the middle is the bridge, and then the pulse engines and the engineering section, and then the cargo area. Shkkka is there, working to fix Electra's Dart ship. I don't tell her that I'm the one who broke it.

You've been on a ship before, right? You know that usually a spaceship is metal-colored and boring white plastic, inside and out. The *Hindsight* is not like that. The corridors are all painted in swirls of bright reds and blues and purples, same as the mess-room, and there are long leafy vines growing along the ceilings. The vines are Telly's—he keeps them watered and healthy green. There are comfy pillows on every chair, and there's always the faint, comforting hum of the ship's engines in the background.

Earlier, Electra called *Hindsight* a *tin-can ship* because from the outside it looks like a cylinder made of scuffed and dented metal.

She's wrong. This ship is not a tin can. It's a bubble of warmth and color and life floating through the darkest, coldest, emptiest places in the galaxy. In this ship, somebody, if they weren't careful, might start to feel like they were *safe*. Like they were at *home*.

For the next week, I do my best to seem quiet and helpful and human and nice and, above all, *normal*.

I am the galley boy, so I use the screen to look up recipes, and then make special meals for each person in the crew. Reetha likes food that is crunchy and salty; Amby prefers things that are mashed up; and Telly, of course, eats only vegetables.

The captain seems to live on bitter kaff and nothing else. She's weary, and spends most of her time on the bridge, checking for blips. She is certain that *Peacemaker* is lurking out there, somewhere. The rest of the crew is snappish too.

It's like they're all waiting for something terrible to happen.

Electra and I spend a lot of time together—without talking. At night she sleeps on the couch, and I scrounge up a pillow and some blankets and sleep on the floor in the galley. The ship's rats aren't happy about this, but really, they shouldn't be in the mess-room anyway.

After a delicious breakfast, I'm busy cleaning—and finishing everybody's eggs and tofu—when Electra jumps up from the couch and starts pacing around the mess-room. She does this a lot.

"Is it time to get tired again?" I ask.

It's been days, and she hasn't once talked to me, so I know she's not going to answer. Instead she casts me a green-eyed glare and then drops to the floor and starts doing this thing where she uses her arms to push herself up and down. It always leaves her sweaty and panting, with her hair-tentacles loose and lashing around her head.

In the galley, I put down the cleaning rag, then hop onto the counter, where I sit cross-legged, watching her.

Finishing her weird arm-pushing thing, she flips over and

starts sitting up and down again and again. Then, to my surprise, she pauses and actually talks to me. "Quit," she pants, "staring at me."

"But what are you *doing*?" I ask. It's weird, right? All this moving around that leaves her exhausted?

Electra jumps to her feet and starts running in place. "Exercising," she says, scowling. "Obviously."

"Can I try?" I ask, hopping off the counter.

She stops, hands on hips, and catches her breath. Her hair-tentacles wave around and then settle onto her shoulders. "One hundred push-ups," she says. She drops to the floor again. "You won't be able to keep up."

Oh, a challenge! "Yes I will!" I answer, and fling myself onto the floor next to her, where I start exercising. And I do keep up. I have lots of extra energy, and I do push-ups with Electra, and then the thing she calls sit-ups, and then a bunch of different exercises that leave her lying flat on the floor, panting. Even her hair-tentacles are lying limp and pale over her shoulders.

"That wasn't so bad," I say, feeling a little hungry.

Electra climbs to her feet, then leans over with her hands on her knees, still panting. Straightening, she brushes her hair-tentacles away from her face, studying me. She frowns. "You're not even tired," she says slowly.

And I have this feeling I've made a terrible mistake.

17

There's an organism called a *slug*. It's a little like my blob of goo form, except that it has its eyes at the end of eyestalks.

Later, while I make dinner for everybody, I feel like Electra has eyestalks and is staring at me in a way that makes me feel prickly all over, even though she's on the other side of the mess-room.

I do my best to ignore her as everybody, including me, gathers around the table and starts to eat. After dinner, I clean up, and the crew leaves the mess-room, and Electra is *still* watching me.

To get away from her, I go into the galley and lie down on the floor. My stomach growls. Electra's been watching me so carefully that I'm not getting enough to eat. Quietly, I sneak a couple of protein bars out of the cupboard.

After a little while, she comes to stand in the doorway of the galley.

Yet another weird thing about humanoids is that they like to begin every conversation by making it clear that neither person is dangerous. They do this by holding out a hand that does not have a weapon in it and shaking the other person's hand, or by smiling, or by exchanging some sort of basically meaningless greeting.

Electra doesn't bother with this.

"It's obvious," she says bluntly.

I'm lying there with about thirty protein bar wrappers scattered around me. "What's obvious?" I ask, and then I burp.

She folds her arms and takes up a wide stance. "I don't know how the crew of this tin-can ship doesn't see it. They must be blind."

I sit up.

"You," she says, pointing at me, "are *not* human."

"Yes," I say firmly, "I am." I'm telling the truth, because at this moment I *am* human.

"No," Electra insists. "You are not. And I can prove it." She reaches into a pocket of her black coverall and pulls out a sleek metal box about the size of her hand.

"What is that?" I ask.

She steps closer, and I scoot away until my back is pressed against a cupboard.

"This," Electra says, holding it up, "is an ID scanner. I

brought it with me from the Dart. At birth, every person in the galaxy is given an identification chip that—"

"I know about ID chips," I interrupt. All the sentient beings in the galaxy have an ID chip that is impossible to remove or alter in any way. The ID chip is scanned every time they get on a ship, or go onto a station or a planet, or go through a doorway or a hatchway, or buy something, or do anything. That means the StarLeague always knows where everybody is.

Except me.

"Stand up," Electra commands in a voice that sounds like she's used to giving orders.

Slowly, I get to my feet. My heart starts to pound—a human reaction.

It means that I'm frightened. When Electra has proof that I have no ID chip, she'll tell the captain. And *then* what will happen? I don't know, but it won't be good.

Electra is wearing a grim and determined look.

And I feel, stirring deep within me, another form that I could take.

All of a sudden, I'm not scared anymore.

Electra holds up the ID scanner. "It doesn't hurt," she says. "Just bend your head. The chip, if you have one, is in the back of your neck."

"No," I tell her, and my voice sounds strange. That other shape stirs within me again, but I hold it back, staying in my human boy form. "I don't think so." Fast as lightning, my hand flashes out and knocks the ID scanner from Electra's grip. It flies across the room, clattering to the floor and coming to rest in a corner.

Electra steps back, swallowing, her eyes wide. She glances at the ID scanner, on the floor across the room, and starts to say something when the door to the mess-room slides open and Captain Astra strides in.

Without hesitating, the captain comes to the counter at the galley. "Eggs," she orders.

I take a deep breath and edge away from Electra. "With—with neon cow powder?" I ask, and my voice shakes a little.

The captain shrugs. "If you insist."

Turning to the counter, I start to make us eggs. Electra watches for a few moments, then crosses to the corner, where she picks up the ID scanner. Then she goes to sit on the couch.

While we eat our snack, the captain is all loungey like her usual self, but she's watching me carefully. I don't ask any questions, or say anything at all.

I am too busy thinking about that other shape, the one I felt stirring inside me, and wondering what it is and why I've never felt it before.

Or maybe I *do* know what it is, and I *have* felt it before.

I just can't remember.

18

The next morning when I make breakfast for everybody, they're all nervous and jangly and snappish, and Electra keeps staring at me. While we eat, the captain talks with Reetha, and I stay quiet and think about memory. When humans think back to *before*, they make a little story out of what happened, with a beginning, a middle, and an end. Not many species do that.

I don't like trying to think about my *before*. All I can remember is floating through space in my blob of goo form. But there had to be something before that. I think it was probably bad.

When everybody finishes eating, the captain stands up and heads for the door.

Before she gets there, Electra follows, grabbing her arm so she can't leave.

"What?" the captain snaps, and pulls her arm away.

Electra leans closer and says something that makes the captain frown and glance at me.

"Yeah, all right," Captain Astra says. With a jerk of her chin, she calls Reetha to her.

Reetha pulls out the key to the restraining cuff and takes it off Electra, and all three of them—the captain, Electra, and Reetha—leave the mess-room, heading toward the bridge.

I know what Electra said to the captain.

I want to talk to you about Trouble.

I have to find out what Electra suspects, and what she knows.

In my rat form, I'm lurking in the ventilation tube, spying on the bridge.

Reetha is at the communications area, and the captain is slouched in her chair with a cup of kaff in her hands, looking tired and a little bit sad.

Electra is standing at attention, and I can't see her face, only the top of her tentacly head. "Permission to report," Electra says.

The captain rolls her eyes and glances at Reetha, over in the communications chair. She does nothing but look blankly back. Then, I notice, Reetha looks up at the ventilation tube. I edge back, just in case I'm visible from the bridge.

"Permission to report," Electra repeats. Because I am getting very good at noticing emotions, I hear that a tinge of annoyance has crept into her voice.

The captain takes a slurp of her kaff. "This isn't a military ship," she says dryly. "You don't have to ask permission before speaking."

Electra gives a little huff of impatience. "Captain Astra, one of your crew is wanted by the StarLeague."

"Reeeeeally," the captain drawls. "Which one?"

"Trouble, the galley boy," Electra says promptly. "An ID scan will prove it."

"My crew," the captain says, "is not your business."

Electra's shoulders hunch, a sign of frustration.

"And anyway," the captain adds, straightening, "we don't have an ID scanner on this ship."

"I have one," Electra says, and pulls the only slightly dented metal box out of her coverall pocket. "General Smag ordered me to pursue your ship because it departed from the station during a hunt for an escaped prisoner. During my mission here I have concluded that this fugitive is, in fact, aboard this ship. You will assist me in arresting it and delivering it to the StarLeague."

"Will I?" the captain asks. "It sounds like you're trying to give me orders," she goes on. "On what is, I remind you, *my ship*." She's starting to sound angry.

"The prisoner is extremely dangerous," Electra insists.

"Trouble is not an escaped prisoner," the captain snaps.

"He's a stowaway, true, but he is completely harmless." She's not relaxed anymore, she's leaning forward in her chair, eyes blazing.

"*And* it is devious," Electra responds.

"Yeah, that's what I've heard," the captain growls. She gets to her feet, still glaring at Electra, who holds her ground.

"You have to help me," Electra says. "It won't let me scan it for its ID chip, and it—"

"Your repeated use of the word *it*," the captain says, and there's no drawl or humor at all in her voice, "is really starting to annoy me."

"It wouldn't let me scan for its ID," Electra goes on doggedly. "It tried to destroy the scanner. But it seems to *like* you, Captain Astra. It will let you do the scan."

The captain glances over at Reetha. "What do you think?"

Reetha looks blankly back at her. Then she glances at the ventilation tube again.

She knows I'm in here. Her chin lifts, and she points with a claw at the door.

Yes, I get it, Reetha. But I can't leave yet.

Earlier the captain said *my crew*, but I know I'm not really part of her crew. I already know what she's going to do.

"I am a StarLeague cadet with orders from General Smag," Electra reminds her. "You must comply with my demands."

The captain sighs and rubs the back of her neck. "All right," she agrees. "We'll get this over with. Reetha, you're with me.

We'll go scan Trouble's ID chip to prove that he's not some kind of intergalactic criminal."

Yes, that's what I thought she'd say.

Before the captain gets to the bridge doorway, I'm skittering along the ventilation tube, heading back to the mess-room. When I get there, I scurry into the galley and shift into my human boy shape. I get to my feet, panting.

They're coming.

Quickly, I pull on my clothes.

The captain is coming, with Reetha, and with Electra. They're going to scan for an ID chip. When she sees that I have no ID chip, the captain will know that I'm not just a stowaway.

But . . . but . . . but . . . if I'm not just a stowaway, what *am* I? I'm a shapeshifter, but am I something else, too? I was so sure that I'm not the escaped prisoner that General Smag is hunting. But what if I'm wrong?

I pace around the mess-room once, twice, taking shaky breaths, my heart pounding and hurting at the same time.

Captain Astra likes the empty space between stars and she is used to being alone. She is not going to help me. She's going to let the StarLeague have me.

It'll only be another second, and they'll come through the door with the ID scanner.

I'm frightened and I'm angry and I'm desperately unhappy and I *hate* all these human feelings!

Then I feel that other shape stirring within me again.

And I'm shaking all over now.

No. *NO.*

The door slides open.

The captain steps into the room, followed by Reetha and Electra.

Run away, Captain Astra! Run! NOW!

And then I shift—

—into a new and extremely deadly and dangerous and terrifying shape.

19

The Hunter is not much bigger than a human boy. But it is far, far more deadly and powerful.

The Hunter's jaws are oversized and low-slung, and its fangs drip with poisonous acid that falls to the deck and starts eating into the metal. Its backbone is ridged with spikes, and smaller, sharper spikes protrude from its double-jointed elbows and shoulders. Its keen eyes and ears can sense every movement and sound, and it smells the delicious scent of fear rising off the female humanoids and the lizardian in the doorway. It is heavily armored, strong, and blindingly fast. It doesn't have any weapons because it doesn't need any. Nothing can hurt the Hunter.

Nothing.

Seeing the Hunter, the old human female flinches, her eyes wide and terrified; at the same moment, the lizardian grabs both of the humanoids' arms and drags them into the corridor. One of them hits a button, and the door slides closed.

The Hunter rams an armored shoulder against the door, and it dents, but holds. From outside the mess-room comes the sound of running feet and shouts.

The Hunter has a target.

It lopes into the food area, shifts into a blob of goo form, and creeps into the handy ventilation tube. Moments later it drops out of the tube into a corridor. As it falls toward the floor, it shifts again into the Hunter form, landing with a heavy thump on its two clawed feet.

The tall blue-skinned humanoid is there. Seeing the Hunter take shape, they emit a high-pitched scream and cower back against the wall.

It would be easy to kill them with a flick of a claw and a quick bite to the neck, but the blue humanoid is not the immediate target. Instead the Hunter darts closer, grabs them as they scream and struggle uselessly, and flings them into the nearest room, hitting the button by the door to seal them in.

The Hunter whirls and continues.

The young female emerges from a doorway bearing a weapon, which she fires. The bolts sizzle down the corridor and whang off the Hunter's armored skin. They are annoying.

She keeps firing as it stalks closer, and then it sweeps her out of the way, continuing toward its target.

The Hunter can hear, in the rest of the ship, shouts and

crashes as the crew reacts to its presence. There is nothing they can do to stop it.

It reaches the bridge. Swiveling its head, it examines the room. Empty. Swiftly, it crosses to the control panel next to the captain's chair. With one blow it smashes it.

Next target, engineering. This ship is *not* continuing to the next station.

The Hunter emerges from the bridge into an empty corridor. The crew has already figured out that hiding is better than trying to attack.

It starts toward the engineering section, knowing the insectoids who run that part of the ship will defend it with their lives. Still, it continues, stalking down the corridor.

And then . . . its stomach gives a mighty growl.

It stops.

Shifting into the Hunter form takes an enormous amount of energy.

It has not had enough to eat lately.

Hungry. The Hunter is *hungry*.

There are plenty of things to eat on this ship.

Before going to deal with the insectoids and engineering, the Hunter will stop at the mess-room and get some food. Something called *stew*, it thinks. And every protein bar left in the galley.

Moving quickly, it follows the corridor to the mess-room. The door opens easily when it hits the button with its claw.

The ship's crew is there, waiting for it.

Humans, the Hunter has learned, think in overcomplicated ways and feel sloppy emotions and do stupid things.

The old woman human is doing something very, very stupid.

Instead of being scared and backing away from the Hunter as it looms in the doorway, she holds her ground. She is probably feeling some kind of complicated human emotion at this moment. Maybe she thinks she can protect her crew.

No matter. To the Hunter, everything is simple: Hunger. Hunt. Kill.

First, the Hunter deals with the others: the lizardian, a tusked humanoid, one of the insectoids, and the girl. As they back away, night-black tentacles erupt from the Hunter's chest and shoulders, hissing around it like snakes. One of them flashes out and knocks the weapon from the girl's hands; other tentacles prison the rest of the crew against a wall.

That leaves the Hunter free to deal with their leader.

It stalks closer. Its arms are long and tipped with razor-sharp claws. They dart out and grab her, lifting her off the ground. She struggles, but it does her no good, because the Hunter is relentless.

It draws her closer. When she speaks, her voice is shaking. "Electra, you can shoot it anytime now."

Oh really? The Hunter snarls into her face. A drop of acid from its fangs drips onto her arm, and she flinches. The Hunter tightens its grip, and she takes a gasping breath.

The Hunter tilts its head, examining its prey closely with one of its eyes. She is an old, tired, lonely, frightened human. She is . . . familiar.

Why?

Because she is an enemy?

No.

Because she likes the darkness of space and thinks that everyone ends up alone.

Midnight snacks and conversation.

Stars that . . .

. . . sing?

Ah. She is the captain.

The Hunter is not going to kill the captain, or damage her. It sets her gently onto the floor.

At the same time, it withdraws the tentacles that are pinning the others against the wall. The Hunter is aware of the girl, Electra, sneakily picking up the weapon from the floor, but the captain raises a hand, holding her in place, and she doesn't fire.

There is a long moment where the captain studies the Hunter. It is not sure what her eyes really see. If they see what the Hunter truly is.

It gazes back at the captain. More than any dog puppy or

blob of goo or human boy, the Hunter is what it is, this hungry shape made for hunting, fighting, killing.

It is devious.

It is trouble.

I am Trouble.

And so I shift back into my human form.

20

The others are on the far side of the mess-room, where Reetha is using a first aid kit to clean and bandage the acid burn on the captain's arm. Electra is holding the weapon, standing guard. The rest of the crew are in other parts of the ship, checking on the damage done by the Hunter.

I am under the table in my human boy shape, curled up in a shivering ball.

Other kinds of beings feel emotions, sometimes very strongly. The bond between insectoids like the Shkkka, who belong to a group mind, is unbreakable and intense. The dog puppy felt emotion, mainly loneliness, but it could feel fear, too. My blob of goo form feels some simple emotions, but only faintly. For example, when Reetha tossed me out the airlock, my dog self was terrified, but after I shifted, my blob of goo shape was not.

My human emotions are different from anything I've felt before, in any form. It's like the way humans experience the taste of food.

I've tasted a lot of different emotions since I stowed away on this ship.

Misery is a new one.

"I want it off this ship," the captain is saying. Then: "Ow!"

"Hold. Still," Reetha says.

"Just get the bandage on," the captain says impatiently. Then I hear the click as Reetha closes the first aid kit.

"I *told* you how dangerous it is," Electra says.

"Yeah, yeah," the captain says. "I want it off this ship *now*."

"It will fight us," Electra warns.

I sit there under the table, shivering. *It.* The captain called me *it*. My stomach growls.

Reetha has gone to one of the lockers, where she gets something; then she starts across the room to my table.

"What are you *doing*?" Electra protests.

Without answering, Reetha shoves a bundle of clothing under the table and goes back to join the others.

With shaking hands, I pull the clothes on. It doesn't stop me from shivering.

"How are we going to get it out of there?" Electra asks in a low voice.

"Ask," Reetha puts in.

"Huh," the captain says, and comes halfway across the

room, where she bends down below the level of the table so she can see me. She straightens quickly. "He's crying."

Electra bends to take a look. "It's trying to manipulate you."

"No," I tell them. "This water is just coming out of my eyes." A drop falls on my hand, and I lick it. Salty. So that's what misery tastes like.

"Come out of there," the captain orders.

I wipe the misery water off my face and crawl out from under the table, getting to my feet.

Electra, her face grim, has her weapon trained on me; Reetha stands with her arms folded across her chest.

The captain studies me, still keeping her distance. "What *are* you?"

"I'm a shapeshifter," I tell her.

"That's become rather obvious," she says.

"I'm the only one." I stare down at my bare toes. "Before I got to the station, I was in my blob of goo shape." I glance up at the captain. "In space. For . . . for a long time." I wrap my arms around myself, but I can't seem to stop shaking. "The blob of goo form doesn't have very much brain, and it forgot what happened to it . . . to me . . . before. Electra's right. I must be the prisoner who escaped from the StarLeague."

"So this blob of goo form of yours can survive outside the ship," the captain notes. "Are you going to resist or attack if we take you to the airlock?"

I can't get my voice to say anything else, so I shake my head, which in human means *no*.

"All right," Electra says. "Let's go." She points with her weapon toward the doorway.

I lead the way out of the mess-room and into the corridor, and in tense silence the others follow.

When we get to the airlock, Electra steps forward and hits a button on the control panel, and the inner hatch door creaks open. "Get in there," she orders.

I don't move.

"Tell it to go in," Electra says to the captain.

Captain Astra is studying me. If she orders me to go into the airlock, I will do it.

"You've seen it," Electra goes on. "You've seen how dangerous it is. From the moment it stepped aboard, it easily could have killed everyone and taken over the ship."

"True," the captain agrees. Then she adds, "But you may have noticed. He didn't."

"I could have," I put in.

She frowns at me.

"You saw it," I say. "The Hunter. Electra is right. It is dangerous."

The captain's frown deepens.

"And devious," I add.

"Don't listen to it," Electra interrupts. "Stop talking," she snaps at me, "and get into the airlock!"

I can't move.

You're always alone in the end.

Space is cold and dark and lonely, and it is silent. Floating out there in my blob of goo form, eventually I will forget everything that happened on this ship. I'll forget the captain, and I'll forget that my name is Trouble.

The captain is still staring at me.

"It's all right," I tell her, wiping my face with the sleeve of my shirt. "It's just this misery water coming out of my eyes."

"Tears, Trouble," she says slowly. "They're called tears."

I look up at the captain. What I expect to see in her eyes is the cold darkness between stars. That's what *should* be there. But it's not.

"Put it out the airlock," Electra snaps.

"No," says the captain, and she almost sounds surprised.

Then Reetha adds, "Our. Trouble." She points a claw at me. She's known for a long time that I'm not really a human boy. I'm surprised she didn't put me out the airlock weeks ago.

And then she adds something completely unexpected.

"Not. Only. Shape. Shifter," Reetha says.

21

Before I can ask Reetha *what* she is talking about—*I'm not the only shapeshifter?!*

—and before Electra can shove me into the airlock herself—

—Telly races down the corridor toward us, his footsteps ringing on the metal deck.

"Captain," he pants, skidding to a stop. He's run all the way here from the bridge. "We just received a broadcast sent to us by the commander of the *Peacemaker*."

Electra immediately stands at attention. "General Smag?"

Telly blinks. "Yes, that's his name." He glances nervously at me, and then away again.

"Innnnteresting," the captain says, drawing out the word. She points with her chin. "Mess-room. Now." She flicks a glance at me. "You too."

When we all get to the mess-room, the captain nods at me and points to a corner.

I sit down there, wrapping my arms around my legs. My stomach is growling. Electra stations herself a few paces away with her weapon out, guarding me.

Captain Astra collapses into a chair and heaves a sigh. "I could use a cup of kaff. So, Telly, what does General Smag want?"

Telly perches on one of the other chairs around the table. "He says we are in imminent danger of attack, that there is a dangerous criminal on our ship." Telly's ears twitch, but he doesn't look toward my corner. "The general orders us to halt where we are and wait, that the *Peacemaker* is coming to rescue us. He says they know exactly where we are."

"*Rats*," the captain curses. Still slouched in her chair, she gazes at me. She's deciding something.

"Captain," Telly says. "The general is waiting for an answer. He says it's urgent."

"You must respond immediately," Electra puts in.

The captain ignores this. "What do you think?" she asks me.

Human brains are funny. I should be reacting to this new information about General Smag, but instead my stomach is growling and my brain is going,

I'm not the only shapeshifter?!

I'm not the only shapeshifter?

I'm not the only shapeshifter!

"Uhhhh," I say slowly.

"Trouble," the captain says sharply.

"What do I think?" I repeat. Well, I'm afraid of General Smag, and I'm also worried about the Hunter, and I'm *hungry*, and part of my brain is *there are other shapeshifters*. But there's something else.

The captain is still gazing at me. "Well?" she asks. "What should we do with you?"

I know what she could lose when the StarLeague arrives and finds me on her ship. Everything. "You don't have any choice." I take a shaky breath. "You'll have to space me and leave me here for the *Peacemaker* to pick up. Or you could hand me over when General Smag gets here."

"Huh," the captain says. Then she speaks to everyone else in the room. "Trouble, yes or no, just offered to give himself up to save the ship. Yes."

"Yes," Reetha agrees.

Shkkka twitches an antenna, which means *yes*.

"Ye-es," Telly says slowly. "He did."

"Oh my," Amby mumbles.

Electra scowls, still holding her weapon as if she's on guard.

The captain turns back to me. "That was a test."

"A test," I repeat.

"You passed," she says.

"How?" I ask, completely confused.

"Figure it out." She leans back in her chair, looking up at

the ceiling, thinking. "I don't want that general near my ship," she says. "We're not responding to his message, and we're not handing Trouble over to him."

"Captain," Electra protests, straightening. "The shapeshifter is a wanted criminal!"

"You keep saying that," Captain Astra says. "What crime, exactly, did he commit?"

"You've seen how dangerous it is," Electra insists.

"You didn't answer my question," the captain drawls. "I'm fairly sure that by the laws of the StarLeague you can't arrest or imprison a person for something he *might* do."

Electra's green eyes blaze with anger and frustration. "It is *not* a person!"

"Ah," the captain says, in complete control. "And that was a test too. You did not pass it, Electra." She jumps to her feet. "Reetha, get me a cup of kaff. We have about five minutes to figure out what we're going to do here."

I know what *I* want to do.

Remember a long time ago when I told you that I am a shapeshifter, and that I am the *only one*? If that's not true—if there really are others like me—it means I'm not alone anymore.

I have no idea if this matters to the captain and everybody else. Still, I have to try. "We have to find the shapeshifters," I say from my corner.

The captain whirls to face me. "What?"

"There are other shapeshifters," I say. "Reetha said there

are, so it must be true. We have to go find them."

"*Do* we?" the captain asks.

Yes. We do. For a long moment I just look at her. At Captain Astra, who used to have a cold darkness in her eyes. She used to think that *You're always alone in the end.*

But she doesn't believe that anymore. I know it. "Can we?" I ask.

The captain takes a deep breath. Then she lets it out. She scrubs both hands through her curly gray hair and then looks at each member of the crew in turn. "Anybody have a problem with this?"

Amby just blinks, but Shkkka twitches an antenna to say *no problem*, and Telly, grinning, says, "Let's do it." Reetha nods.

"All right," the captain says. "This is what we're going to do. Assuming that rat-bit stealth-box is ready?" she asks, with a glance at Shkkka.

"It'ssss ready," Shkkka answers.

"*Finally*," the captain says.

"What *is* a stealth-box?" I put in. I know it's something Shkkka has been working on for the past week. "Is it some kind of ultra-top-secret sneak device?"

The captain grins widely. "Hah. Yes. It bends a pocket of space around us, like a little hiding place. Very useful, if often out of commission."

"How does it work?" I ask.

"Science," the captain says with a shrug. "Shkkka and

Reetha understand it. Anyway, assuming it works properly, we'll hide in our little pocket of space, and when *Peacemaker* gets here, we will be long gone *and* untraceable."

"Where are we going?" I ask.

The captain shakes her head as if I'm being stupid. "To find the shapeshifters."

"No, you are not," Electra announces, raising her weapon. Suddenly she looks grim and dangerous. "Everybody against the wall," she orders. "I am taking over this ship until General Smag arrives."

"Wait," I say, getting up from my place in the corner.

When I move, everyone in the room freezes, staring at me.

Then Electra turns, grips her weapon with both hands, and aims it at me. "Stay back," she snaps.

She's being brave, but she's also being stupid. "Electra," I protest.

She grits her teeth. "I am a StarLeague Dart pilot. I don't have any choice. Now put your hands up. I don't want any trouble from you."

"Trouble is what you've got," I say, and as I speak, my voice turns raspy, and before she can fire the weapon, I've shifted—in a flash—into the Hunter again. In one mighty bound, I'm across the room, ripping the weapon from Electra's hand, crumpling it, and dropping it to the floor.

Then I shift back and I'm standing there, barefoot, and the crew is all cowering away, even though I'm in my human shape again. Electra glares at me, and her hair tentacles lash angrily around her head.

The captain recovers. "Go, uh . . ." She waves a shaking hand at me. "Go put your clothes back on, Trouble."

Feeling a little shaky myself, I go back to my corner and get dressed, while Reetha seizes Electra roughly, pulls the ID scanner out of the pocket of her coverall, and drops it into her own pocket. Then Reetha puts a menacing claw on Electra's shoulder. "Space 'er?" she asks.

I finish pulling a shirt over my head. "No!" I say.

"Trouble, you don't know about these Dart pilots," the captain says. "They're fanatically loyal and trained from birth to be deadly. She has to go."

I stay where I am and say carefully, "Electra's a kid."

"She's trouble," the captain warns.

"Yes, she is," I agree. "But she's a person."

Electra is staring at me, as if she's surprised that I don't want to toss her out into space. Her face is pale and her hair-tentacles are drained of color. She's scared.

"If you put Electra out the airlock," I remind the captain, "she will get *ebullism* and die."

"All right," the captain says, and blows out a frustrated breath. "Fine. We won't space her." Then she turns to Reetha. "You said there are other shapeshifters. Where do we have to go to find them?"

Reetha, it turns out, doesn't know.

22

After Captain Astra growls at Reetha for not knowing where we need to go to actually find the other shape-shifters, they hurry off to the bridge to get the stealth-box set up and to tell Amby to plot a new course. Telly goes out after putting the restraining cuff onto Electra again.

And then Electra and I are alone in the mess-room.

My brain is still bouncing around inside my skull because of everything that has happened, but above all I'm *starving*, so I go to the galley. I don't bother making the stew properly, I just open the packets and dump them straight into my mouth. At the same time, I'm ripping open protein bars and gulping them down. Then I eat half of the lettuce from Telly's garden, including the roots.

Once I've taken the edge off my hunger, I go out to the

mess-room because I want to talk to Electra. I have *so* many questions for her. I flop onto the floor with a pile of protein bars on my belly.

But before I can start, she asks *me* a question.

Her face is still very pale, only green around the edges, and her hair-tentacles are pale and droopy. She's sitting on the couch, not far away. "It was you," she says, her voice bitter. "Wasn't it? You attacked my Dart ship and damaged it so that I was captured?"

"Yep," I say, and take a bite of protein bar.

She makes a disgusted sound. "I can't believe what an idiot I am."

"No you're not," I protest.

"I had a mission," she says savagely. "I made a stupid assumption that this stupid ship was harmless, and now I'm paying for it, all right? So just shut up about something you don't know anything about."

So grumpy. Maybe she's hungry. "Want a protein bar?" I ask her.

"No," she mutters. "I do not want a stupid protein bar."

I sit up. Since she's actually talking to me for once, I might as well try asking some questions. "Do you know where I escaped from?" I ask. "I mean, you saw the Hunter, right? What kind of place could hold me?"

She gives half a shrug. "A class-four military prison could." She gnaws on a thumbnail. "Actually no. It didn't, obviously. I don't know where the prison was. The StarLeague keeps the location of all of its prisons secret, for obvious reasons." Then she glares at me. "I shouldn't even be talking to you, criminal."

I don't remember if I'm a criminal or not, so I don't bother arguing with her about it. Instead I get to my feet and go to a locker. Taking out the remote, I bring up a cookbook on the screen. "What species of humanoid are you?" I ask.

"Why do you want to know?" she asks suspiciously.

"You'll see," I promise.

"Tintaclodian," she answers.

I blink.

She reaches up and wraps one of her hair-tentacles around a finger. "We're called that because of our tintacles."

"Not *tent*acles?" I ask.

"No." The tentacle around her finger turns darker blue, then black, then a murky green, and then it goes blue again. "They change color. Tint. Tintacles."

"They show how you're feeling," I say.

"Sometimes," she says, and then looks away.

I look up *tintaclodians* in the cookbook. It says that Electra's species likes eating insects, among other things. "What's *grasshopper*?" I ask her, studying a recipe. "Is it a kind of vegetable?"

She doesn't answer. Instead she gets to her feet and stomps away, muttering to herself. After a minute, she stomps back, her tintacles waving angrily around her head.

"All right," she growls. "Fine." She glares at me.

"What?" I prompt.

She gives an exasperated sigh. "Thank you," she says through gritted teeth, "for not letting the captain put me out an airlock."

I can't help it—I smile at her. She's so polite! "You're welcome."

I find myself feeling strange, complicated human emotions about Electra. At the same time that I feel dislike toward her because she's grumpy and she called me a *thing* and *it* and doesn't think I'm a person, I feel something else about how brave and determined she is. I think it might be *like*.

Electra flops onto the couch and stares at the ceiling. I eat five more protein bars and don't talk to her, because I can tell she needs to do some thinking. And then the captain hurries back into the mess-room with Reetha. "Search her," she orders, pointing at Electra.

Electra stands still while Reetha goes through her pockets. "What are you looking for?" she asks.

The captain scowls at her. "You've been signaling to General Smag, haven't you?"

Electra blinks. Her tintacles turn pink.

"I think that means she's surprised," I point out.

"So you *haven't* been signaling the general," Captain Astra concludes.

"Nothing," Reetha reports, finished with her search.

"Rats," the captain curses. "We've checked the Dart ship, too, and there's no tracking device. So, before we switched on the stealth-box, how was Smag able to follow us?" She narrows her eyes. "Do you know?" she asks Electra.

Electra's hair-tintacles turn muddy brown. "No," she snaps. "But it doesn't matter. General Smag is relentless. Now that he knows the criminal is on board, he will never stop pursuing you. This tin-can ship will not escape the StarLeague military. When you are caught, you will all go to prison." She turns her glare on me. "And it will be entirely your fault."

"Maybe they won't catch us," I say.

"They will," she promises. "*Peacemaker* is coming. Even with that stupid stealth-box, there is no escape."

"But maybe there is," I say.

"Ugh!" Electra huffs out a disgusted breath. "Why am I even talking to you?"

"I don't know," I tell her. "You said you weren't going to."

The captain rolls her eyes. "Enough arguing." She points at Electra. "You stay here." She points at me. "And you come with us."

I follow her and Reetha out of the mess-room. They know there's no point in putting a restraining cuff on me, but, the captain says, they do not want me roaming around the ship. So they're going to lock me up.

"But—" I start to say, to remind them that I must have, after all, escaped from a class-four military prison. I don't know exactly what that means, but I doubt anything on this ship can hold me.

"I don't want to hear it," the captain interrupts. Keeping her distance, she leads me out of the mess-room and along the corridor to the crew's sleeping rooms. Reetha follows. We get to a door; the captain taps a button to open it. Inside is a small room. Its walls are painted dark blue, and there are no blankets or pillows on the narrow bed. "Go on in there," she orders.

"But—" I start to say again, because we haven't talked about where we're going to find the shapeshifters, which is what we're supposed to be doing, right?

"Trouble," she says impatiently, "*Peacemaker* and General Smag are out there somewhere and I have our escape to plan and a very temperamental stealth-box to do it with. I don't have time to deal with you right now."

I step into the room.

A second later the door slides shut behind me. I immediately try to open it again from the inside, but I can't. They locked me in.

23

I sit down on the bed.

All right. I will be normal and good. The captain is busy and she doesn't want me roaming around the ship, so I'll stay here.

I lie down and look at the ceiling. It is painted dark blue too, and it has tiny stars stuck all over it. The room smells like cleaning chemicals. I can hear the soothing hum that is always in the background on this ship.

Electra is so sure that *Peacemaker* is coming after us. General Smag, she said, is *relentless*.

I can just picture the huge StarLeague military ship following us. Like a . . .

Do you know what a shark is? Sea creature, lots of teeth? Yes?

Peacemaker is like a shark, swimming through the deepest

darkness of space. A huge, terrifying predator. And *Hindsight* is an awfully small fish.

My stomach growls, distracting me. "I know," I tell it. Soon the captain will remember that I need to eat a lot, and Reetha or somebody will come with six bowls of stew and a pile of protein bars, and maybe even dessert.

I fall asleep thinking about food, and when I wake up, it seems like a long time since I last ate, and I am very, very, very, very, very, *very* hungry.

The captain put me in here, but she didn't actually say that I had to *stay* in here.

"Trouble," I say warningly to myself.

As an answer, my stomach growls loudly at me.

"I can't argue with that," I reason, and shift into my blob of goo form. Extending my pseudopods, I crawl up the wall to a grated vent at the edge of the ceiling. I ooze through it, then shift into a rat. In that form, I scurry along until I find another grate, shift and ooze through it, and come out in a corridor, where I have barely enough energy left to shift into my human boy shape.

The red-painted door of the mess-room is only a few steps away. I hit the button to open it and peer inside.

The only person there is Electra, asleep on the couch. Quietly, I go to the galley and get a few protein bars, and I also grab a coverall out of a locker and put it on, because humans don't like it when other humans are not wearing clothes.

Leaving the mess-room, I pad barefoot down the corridors until I get to the bridge. The doorway is open, and I go in.

The captain is slouched in her scruffy chair next to the control panel, which has a dent in it with bits of broken plastic and wire sticking out. She's the only one there.

Seeing me, she gets to her feet. "Trouble," she says warily.

I hold up the protein bars. "Midnight snack?"

Her eyes narrow. Slowly, she sits back down in her chair. "I have to keep reminding myself that you're not human. You're not what you look like."

I tell her what I keep telling myself: "No matter what shape I'm in, I'm always me."

"The Hunter is you?" she asks.

My blob of goo form does this thing when it's in deepest space. It pulls in all of its pseudopods and shuts down most of its senses and its surface hardens, like rock.

My human body wants to do the same thing. I crouch and wrap my arms around my knees, making myself small. "Trouble is me," I say quietly. "And the Hunter is me."

"Hmmm," the captain says. "Why did the Hunter come to the mess-room?"

"I was hungry," I whisper.

"Heh. That's what I thought." The captain leans over to look at me, her elbows on her knees. "You know, Trouble, I've been sitting here thinking about what happened. And I realized that you scared us all, but you didn't actually hurt anyone, and you didn't even do that much damage to the ship." She straightens. "Let's see. You dented the mess-room door. You terrified Amby. You smashed the control table here, next to my chair." She pulls at one of the wires protruding from the panel. "What you didn't know is that it doesn't work anyway. I only use it for holding a cup of kaff."

I extend a pseudopod—a leg, I mean—and climb to my feet. "An old moldy cup of kaff," I say.

"In fact," the captain concludes, "Electra did more damage shooting at you than the Hunter did."

"Do you think Electra's right?" I blurt out. "Will General Smag catch us and send us all to prison?"

The captain gives a lazy smile. "They won't catch us so easily. We've used the stealth-box before, Trouble. This isn't the first time we've had to stay hidden from the StarLeague."

"Waaaaait," I say slowly, figuring something out that I should have figured out before. "You . . . this ship. You left the station in a hurry. I was there when you gave the order to close the outer hatch. You said . . ." I remember it, me in my dog puppy shape, crouched behind a pile of junk in the corridor. "You said you didn't want the StarLeague officer poking his nose around in your ship." I shake my head. "All of that had nothing to do with me."

"Ah!" The captain taps her nose. I have no idea what it means. "Go on," she says.

I feel something bubbling up in my chest. It's something

dogs don't do, and neither do blobs of goo. It's a laugh. I clap both hands over my mouth to keep it from getting out.

The captain raises an eyebrow.

And I can't help it—the laugh bursts out. "*You* are a criminal!" I say.

"*Criminal*," she scoffs. "That's not a very good word for what we do."

"What *do* you do?" I ask, and I suddenly hope it's not something bad that hurts other people. But I know the captain, and I don't think that it is.

She smiles in a familiar way. For an instant she looks like *The Lady*. "We have regular cargo, and we trade between stations like an ordinary ship, and when the StarLeague is watching, we obey StarLeague laws. But sometimes we go to the darkest places between stars, and we switch on the stealth-box, and we wait in our little hidden pocket of space. There are people who, for various reasons, refuse to live under the strict rule of the StarLeague. People who desperately need supplies—seeds or medicine or farm equipment, things like that—and they meet us in those in-between places. When we've unloaded our cargo, we continue to the station."

"You're devious," I say.

"We certainly are," the captain agrees.

"Even more devious than I am," I say.

"I doubt," the captain says dryly, "that is possible."

24

The captain tells me to go back to my room. "And once you're in there, stay there," she orders. "I don't need you underfoot."

I gather up the protein bars. "Where are we going, exactly?" I ask.

"Ah," Captain Astra says. "You have a question, right?"

"I have a lot of questions," I say. Where did I come from? Why was I in a StarLeague prison? What will happen the next time I turn into the Hunter? Is it true that cheese powder is made out of neon cows? Will Electra ever stop disliking me? Why is *The Lady* smiling? Do stars really sing?

"I'll bet you do," the captain says. "But the main one."

My main question is whether there are others like me somewhere in the galaxy. "We're going to find the shapeshifters, right?"

"We are," the captain says.

"Have you figured out where they are?" I ask, and inside me I feel a strange bubble of excitement and hope and terror and happiness.

"No," the captain says. Before the happy-bubble inside me can pop, she goes on. "Not yet. For now, thanks to the stealth-box, we're hidden from *Peacemaker* and General Smag. Once we're sure we're safe, there's a place we can go to find out where the shapeshifters are. There is something called The Knowledge, which knows everything about everything in the entire galaxy."

"The Knowledge," I repeat. "Is it a computer?"

"I'm not sure what it is," the captain says. "We are going to ask it your question, and we will get an answer." She tells me that The Knowledge inhabits an asteroid that orbits a weak star that isn't too far from our current location. "Amby should be able to set a direct course," she goes on. "It'll take us about two days to get there."

And then an alarm goes off and the captain shoots to her feet. "What?!" she exclaims, and then goes to the communications station, where she peers at a screen. "*Peacemaker*," she says, and makes it sound like a curse. "There is no *way* they could be tracking us." She punches a few buttons and gives a frustrated curse. "But somehow they're tracking us."

A creepy coldness crawls up my spine. Worry, I think. "Will they catch us before we get to The Knowledge?"

"Not if I have anything to do with it," she mutters. Then she points at the door. "On your way back to your room, tell Reetha that I need her on the bridge. Now!"

Quickly and quietly, I make my way from the bridge to the room where Reetha sleeps.

Except, it turns out, lizardians don't sleep.

When I tap on the door to see if she's there, it slides open immediately, and Reetha looms in the doorway, staring down at me. I'm standing in the dim corridor, the pockets of my coverall stuffed full of protein bars, the metal floor cold under my bare toes.

She folds her arms. "What."

"The captain wants you on the bridge," I tell her. "The *Peacemaker* changed course and is tracking us again."

She nods and starts to push past me.

"Reetha," I say, and she pauses. "I have some questions for you. It'll only take a minute."

"Ask," Reetha says in a low voice.

"Well," I say. "You've known for a while that I'm a shapeshifter. Why didn't you tell the captain? Why didn't you space me? Do you even like me? It's hard to tell."

Reetha huffs out a frustrated sigh. Then she reaches up with a claw and taps her own ridged forehead. "Not. Human."

I blink. Of course. I have taken the shapes of other species before, and they have their own ways of thinking. Reetha has her own lizardian reasons for what she does.

And, I think, more than anybody else on this ship, Reetha sees me. She sees *me*.

I wait, but she doesn't add anything. "I have one more question," I say. "How did you know that there are other shapeshifters in the galaxy?"

Reetha stares unblinking at me with her golden eyes. "Screen." Then she leaves, heading for the bridge.

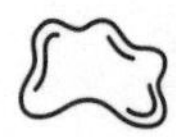

I know, I know. I told the captain that I would go straight back to my room. Instead I head to the mess-room so I can look up *shapeshifters* on the screen, just as Reetha told me to do.

The mess-room is quiet and dark. Electra is lying on the couch, asleep.

I sneak across to a locker and get the remote, and then I drag Amby's nest-chair into the middle of the room. After climbing into it, I push the button on the remote, scrolling through until I find the information I'm looking for displayed in big pictures on the screen.

It turns out that humans, at least, have things called *legends* and *myths* about shapeshifters. There are stories about humans who can change into animals, or about demons—evil creatures—that can change into just about anything and do things like eat hearts and livers and drown humans and drink their blood.

The *nāga* is sometimes a snake that has the face of a human, and sometimes a human with snakes growing out of their neck.

As I'm watching a picture of a *nāga* on the screen, I realize that Electra is awake and sitting up on the couch. She doesn't say anything as the next shapeshifter appears. It's a *selkie*, which is a mammal called a *seal* that can become human if they take off their seal skin. I can't quite figure out how they manage this. It must be messy.

Electra and I keep on watching. The *kitsune*, we learn, is a fox that can turn into a human. The legends say that the *kitsune* is always hungry and eats a lot. Hmmm.

Another kind of shapeshifter is a human person called a *prince* who is turned into a *frog* and then back again by a kiss.

Did you already know about *kissing*? It's when humans, for emotional reasons, touch their lips to another human's lips. I keep thinking I've found out the weirdest thing about humans, and then there's something even weirder.

The screen goes dark. I turn it off and get to my feet.

Electra, on the couch, stays quiet.

There wasn't all that much information about shapeshifters, but suddenly I feel sure that if the captain is sneaky enough and The Knowledge is helpful enough and if we can stay ahead of *Peacemaker* and not get arrested by General Smag and put on trial by the StarLeague and tossed into a secret class-four military prison . . .

. . . we *are* going to find them.

25

I'm hoping we managed to get away from the *Peacemaker* again. There's nothing I can do to help with that, so I do what the captain ordered—I go back to the little room with 147 stars on the ceiling.

I intend to stay there—I really do!

But being lonely, it turns out, is even worse than being hungry. I last about another day—we should be almost to The Knowledge's asteroid—when I can't stand it anymore.

Escaping the second time is just as easy as it was the first time. After oozing out, I shift into my human shape and lope along to the mess-room and poke my nose in.

Electra is on the floor doing push-ups. Seeing me, she pauses. "You."

"Yep," I say.

"You're not wearing any clothes," she notes.

"They don't come with me when I shift," I tell her.

Then Amby comes out of the galley, holding a bowl of food. Seeing me, their eyes go wide, they shriek and drop the bowl, and stew splatters around their feet.

I edge into the mess-room and close the door behind me. "Hello," I say.

Amby is backing away, their long fingers over their chest to calm themself. "I'd better . . . Oh no. This is . . . well." The backs of their legs hit the couch, and they fold up, shivering a little.

I feel shivery too, and it's not just because it's cold in the mess-room and I'm not wearing any clothes. Amby's the one who told me about *family* and *home*, and now they are afraid of me.

After getting some clothing from a locker and putting it on—just a big shirt that must belong to Reetha, because it hangs down to my knees—I head for the galley, where I grab some cleaning spray and a cloth. "Don't worry, Amby," I say as I kneel on the floor to wipe up the spilled stew. "I'm not going to bother you."

Electra has gotten to her feet and is leaning to the side, stretching her muscles. "You're already bothering them," she says. "Almost as much as you're bothering me."

"Sorry," I say. "I got hungry."

"Oh, what a surprise," Electra says.

"And lonely," I add.

She doesn't say anything about that.

Finished cleaning up the floor, I go to the galley, where I roll up my sleeves and start concocting a kind of dessert food called *cake*. To make it, you combine basic baking mix from a packet and egg powder from another packet and water, and stir it up really well, and then it sets for about a minute, and it's cake.

"What are you doing?" Electra calls.

"Cooking," I say.

"*Why?*" she asks.

I poke my head out of the galley. "It's my job."

"No it's not," she shoots back.

"Yes it is," I say happily, and start stirring the cake mix.

"This is a stupid argument," she grumbles. "Isn't it?" she asks Amby, who is still sitting on the couch.

"I . . . I don't . . ." Amby says faintly.

I put the cake aside to set, and start looking through the cabinets to see if we have any *grasshoppers*, whatever they are, for Electra's cake.

I hear footsteps and look up to find that Electra has come up to the counter.

"I can't believe *Peacemaker* and General Smag haven't caught us yet," she says.

Us, she said. That's interesting. "Captain Astra is devious," I tell her.

She leans on the counter. "You are *all* devious."

At that I look up at her and grin, and in response her tintacles go from green to purple, and they wave around her head. She doesn't smile back at me, though; she scowls.

I wonder if she still thinks that I'm not a person.

The cake is ready, so I get out a knife to cut it, and put a piece on a plate and give it to her. "Here. It's chocolate."

Amby is still sitting on the couch, looking from me to Electra and back again with wide eyes.

I give them my nicest, most normal smile. "Do you want a piece of cake? It's delicious."

"Well," Amby says, and I can see that they are trying to be brave. "I think . . . yes. I rather would." They come over to the counter and let me hand them a plate of cake.

Then I ask Electra, "Do you know if *Peacemaker* is still tracking us?"

She's silent for a moment. Then she says, "They were talking about it at breakfast. Apparently the stealth-box is working properly." She glances over at Amby. "Isn't that right?"

Amby nods. "Yes. We should . . . Well, you know, we should be able to avoid being detected. There is no . . . no way for them to track us."

Then I ask them if they will tell me about their family and their home planet, because I want to hear about it again and Electra hasn't heard it in the first place.

"I don't need to hear about Amby's family," Electra says. She has cake crumbs on her face, and she's frowning. "Or their home."

"Yes, you do," I tell her. "Go ahead, Amby."

They blink and set their cake plate on the counter. "Well . . ."

"Please?" I ask.

"All right." Leaving their cake uneaten, they settle onto the couch, next to Electra, and I sit on the floor, and Amby tells about their parental units, and about their home in a cozy nest high up in a tree, and their many pod-siblings. As they talk about their family, I can see that Amby misses them all a lot. I lean against the couch, listening, and I can imagine what their home planet was like. At the end of the story, Amby falls silent for a few moments. "But now, you know," Amby adds at last, "the *Hindsight* is my home." I feel the faintest, feather-light touch of their hand on the top of my head. "And," they go on, "it is home . . . Well, it is home for the rest of the crew too."

Then Captain Astra rushes into the room, interrupting. "To the bridge, Amby," she barks, and then glowers at me.

"*P-Peacemaker*?" Amby quavers, getting to their feet.

"Yeah," the captain says, heading out the door again. "I have no idea how the StarLeague is tracking us, but somehow they've picked us up again. We have got to shake them before we get to The Knowledge."

26

Banished to my room again, I lie on the bed and listen to the pulse engines humming and stuttering, and for a while they roar, as if the *Hindsight* is in a huge hurry. My guess is that it's more evasive maneuvers, trying to escape the relentless General Smag. It's better for me to stay out of the way while this is happening—I make the rest of the crew nervous. I know for sure that even chocolate cake and a pat on the head can't make Amby stop seeing the Hunter when they look at me.

To pass the time, and to try to keep from feeling too worried, I count the stars on the ceiling again.

And I try to imagine what it'll be like when The Knowledge answers my question and we find the other shapeshifters. I wonder what a shapeshifter place might be like. Will it be like Amby's home planet? Will there be people who are like me and who aren't scared of me? Plenty of food? Warmth and color and interesting conversations? Safety? Home? Family?

But what if it's not like that at all?

The pulse engines shut down. The ship goes silent.

We must have reached The Knowledge.

"Reetha," I ask as she opens the door to let me out, "what emotion is it when you feel shaky in your stomach and you can't sit still and your thoughts keep spinning off in all directions?"

She shrugs. "Human."

I am feeling very *human* about this meeting with The Knowledge.

Reetha takes me to the mess-room. There, Electra and the crew, except for the captain, are waiting for a message from The Knowledge.

As I come in, they all stare at me. Electra's tintacles are muddy green, and she has them tied with a string so they can't escape and flutter around her face.

"Hello," I say, and give half a wave.

None of them say *hello* back to me. They all watch carefully as I cross the room to my corner, where I lean against the wall.

After a short while the captain hurries in. She spots me at once. "Good, you're here." Then she turns to address the others. "The Knowledge has given us permission to fly the Dart to its asteroid." She frowns. "It wants me, the 'StarLeague cadet,'"—she nods at Electra—"and our 'passenger,' which is Trouble, obviously."

"Why does it want me?" Electra asks from where she's standing at attention not far from me. Then she adds, "How does it even know that I'm being held prisoner on this ship?"

"That's what The Knowledge does," the captain answers. "It knows."

She gives orders for the crew to stay alert and for Shkkka to have the ship ready to depart as soon as we return from the asteroid. We can't stay here for too long, she says. Even though the *Hindsight* is hidden in one of the stealth-box's space-pockets, General Smag is out there—searching for us.

After taking the restraining cuff off Electra's wrist, the captain leads us to the cargo bay, where Electra's Dart has been stored.

It's sleek and silver and it fills up almost the entire space. Thanks to Shkkka, the damage I did has been fixed. The captain pushes a button and a hatch slides open.

Before we step inside, the captain stops, turning to Electra. "Star League Cadet," she says.

"Ye-es?" Electra says slowly. She was looking at the Dart with shining eyes—now she turns to answer the captain.

Captain Astra points at me. "That is a dangerous shape-shifter." She leans closer, speaking right into Electra's face. "Behave yourself. Try to escape or alert General Smag or do anything that I don't order you to do, and I'll send Trouble after you, and believe me, you will regret it."

"A threat," Electra says bitterly.

The captain straightens. "Yes. A threat."

"Fine," Electra says.

"Good," the captain says.

They glare at each other for another moment. Then we all climb into the Dart. The pilot's seat is surrounded by blinking lights, buttons, switches, screens, scrolling information. The captain slides into it. Electra sits in a narrow seat behind it, and I sit on the floor nearby.

"Huh," the captain says. She reaches out and pushes a button. Nothing happens. She pushes another button, and the outer hatch closes. She flips a switch, and the Dart lurches up, bashes against a wall of the cargo bay, and, with a rattling thump, lands on the deck.

"Are there seat belts on this ship?" I ask Electra, rubbing a bump on my head.

"Usually they're not needed," she answers. Then she calls, "Do you want me to fly the Dart, Captain, since I actually know how?"

The captain turns in her seat, looking annoyed. "That must be why The Knowledge wanted you along."

They switch places, Electra slithering past the captain to get into the pilot seat. Quickly, she powers up the Dart.

I watch out the front window as the big hatchway at the end of the *Hindsight* opens, revealing stars, darkness, and a distant sun. Gently, the Dart lifts from the deck and eases out into space. Once we're outside, the asteroid comes into view.

Usually an asteroid is a big chunk of lumpy dead rock drifting in space.

The Knowledge's asteroid is like that, but it's bristling with antennae spires and dishes and a gleaming ansible port—all of this for receiving information, and for sending it out, too, to appear on screens all over the galaxy. My guess is that we have to come here ourselves instead of sending a message because the StarLeague is monitoring all communications to The Knowledge, and a question about shapeshifters will bring them here as fast as the *Peacemaker* can travel.

Electra brings the Dart around to the shadowed side of the asteroid, and maneuvers it into a narrow docking area. A hatch closes behind us. Everything is dark except for the blue lights on the control panel.

My human heart goes *ka-thump-thump-thump*. We're here.

27

Following the captain, we climb out of the Dart. The darkness is a heavy black blanket.

For some reason, it makes me want to whisper. "I can shift into a shape that can see in the dark," I offer.

"No need," the captain says loudly. "Look."

After a moment my human eyes adjust, and I catch sight of a glow in the distance.

Without speaking, the three of us head in that direction.

We walk for what seems like a long time through a dark tunnel as the glow gets brighter and brighter.

At last it gets so bright that my eyes are dazzled as we step into an open space. I blink at the brightness until I can see that we're standing on a small flat place; the rest of the room is spherical, as if it's been hollowed out of the middle of the asteroid, and the curved walls are made of light. The walls pulse with a deep, rhythmic thrum.

There's a whirring sound, and a little door opens in the light. A small shiny orb darts out. It flits past the captain, past Electra, and then buzzes around me.

"What is it?" I ask.

"An eye," the captain answers. "It belongs to The Knowledge—it has trillions of them, all over the galaxy. It's using the eye to look at us up close. Just stay still."

The Knowledge examining me with its eye makes me feel prickly all over.

Then another door opens in the light, and a long, thin metal appendage extends. At its end is a sharp needle—before I can dodge, it pokes me in the arm, drawing a bit of blood out of me. At the same time, another metal appendage with scissors at its end shoots out and takes a snip of my hair.

"Stop that!" the captain snaps.

Both appendages retreat into their doors in the light-walls.

The *thrum-thrum-thrum* in the room gets louder.

When The Knowledge speaks, its voice comes from all around us, and it is so deep, it rumbles in my bones. My human body has a strange reaction to it—all of my hair stands up on end, and tiny bumps break out on the surface of my skin.

A glance to the side shows me that Electra and Captain Astra are having similar reactions: their eyes are wide, and I see Electra give a shiver.

Greetings, The Knowledge says.

"Hello," I answer.

Electra gives me a wild look. "Shhhhh," she hisses. Her tintacles are quivering and have turned yellow.

The shiny orb-eye bobs over to the captain.

Captain Astra of the Hindsight, The Knowledge says. *Long-haul space trader, human, known to frequent the IoY4456z region of the galaxy.*

"Sounds about right," the captain says.

The eye circles Electra. *Senior StarLeague Cadet Electra Zox. Tintaclodian. Top Dart pilot in your class, destined for greatness within the StarLeague military complex.*

Electra's only response to this is a curt nod.

The eye moves on, floating before me. In its curved surface, I can see a roundy, stretched-out reflection of me. "That wasn't very polite," I tell it, "poking and snipping at me like that."

The eye comes closer, then retreats again, as if it's fascinated by me.

They call you Trouble, The Knowledge says.

"That's my name," I tell it.

The samples taken—blood from your arm, hair from your head—indicate that you are human.

"I am human when I'm in this shape," I tell it.

I hear a surprised gasp from the captain.

Shift, The Knowledge orders. *Information must be gathered. More samples must be taken.*

"No," the captain snaps. "Leave him alone."

The Knowledge's thrum takes on a threatening edge.

"Wait," I tell it. I consider the request. There is only one Knowledge. It has a purpose, and that's to collect information. It probably can't help but ask for every scrap that it can get. "I will shift," I tell it, "if you're polite about it."

There is a deep *thrum, thrum* from the walls. Then it says, *Please.*

I haven't told you yet what it feels like to shift from one shape to another, or what it looks like.

When I shift, it's like I give a signal, and it goes into every cell of me—or whatever it is that I'm made up of. Goo, maybe. And down at that microscopic level there's a change that ripples through me. It happens fast, in an instant. To somebody watching, it looks like I blur from one shape into the next, in an eyeblink.

I can't shift into a *selkie* or a *nāga* or a *kitsune*. But I can shift into a lizardian or an insectoid, and into animals like the dog and the rat, and a lot of others. And the Hunter. I don't know why I can shift into the things that I can, and can't shift into the things that I can't. It's like . . . I don't remember the shapes, but somehow, my body remembers.

When I shift into them, I *become* them.

Even though I am also still me.

As The Knowledge requested, I shift into another form. The change ripples through me, and a blink later I'm my dog puppy self. I feel the cold floor under my paws; looking up, I see the captain and Electra staring down at me. They are shades of gray-blue to my dog eyes, and my keen dog nose smells that they're both on the edge of frightened. Of me or The Knowledge, I'm not sure which. Maybe both.

My dog puppy self starts panting, but I keep still as the appendages extend from their little doors again and poke me for a bit of blood and for a snip of puppy fur.

As they retreat into the glowing walls, I shift back into my human boy form and put on my clothes again.

The silvery round eye watches me the whole time.

Canine species, The Knowledge says. *Breed: mongrel.*

"Yep," I say.

You give off a unique energy when you shift, The Knowledge notes. *Now shift into the other*, it says. It means the Hunter.

"No," I tell it.

Please it adds.

"No," I repeat.

The *thrum-thrum* deepens again. It must be the sound of The Knowledge thinking.

Finally it says, *You have a question.*

The captain releases a relieved breath. "Yes, we have a question," she says. And then, instead of asking it, she waits.

You wish to know where the other shapeshifters can be found, The Knowledge says.

My heart gives a *ka-thump*, because The Knowledge

knows. There truly are shapeshifters out there somewhere.

"Yes," the captain answers. "We want to find them for Trouble."

There is an answer to that question, The Knowledge says in its deep, thrumming voice. *To hear the answer, you must complete a task.*

"What!?" Electra interrupts, her voice outraged. "You're not going to just tell us?"

I cast her a surprised glance. Electra with the *us* again.

The Knowledge ignores her. *Agreed?* it asks.

"All right," the captain says warily. "What's the task?"

Instead of us getting an answer, a silvery web erupts from the wall, flies across the room, and wraps around the captain, and as she lets out a yell of surprise, it drags her away, out of reach.

28

The captain is pinned high against the curve of the wall of light, struggling against the silvery webs that hold her fast.

Beside me, Electra is crouched, reaching for a weapon that she isn't actually carrying.

And me—I see my captain, in danger. Down deep, I feel the Hunter stirring.

Do not move, booms out the voice of The Knowledge.

I freeze, still in my human shape, and so does Electra.

The captain rips out a series of words that I suspect are profanity, until a metal appendage emerges from the wall and slaps a bandage over her mouth.

"Let her go!" I shout.

When you have completed the task, The Knowledge says.

"No," I say. "Just let her go, and we'll leave."

Captain Astra agreed, says The Knowledge.

"It's true," Electra puts in, her voice tense. "She did."

I glance aside, and see that she has her grim, determined face on, and her tintacles are gray. I look up at the captain, who is furious behind the bandage that prevents her from speaking. "You think we don't have a choice?" I ask.

Electra shakes her head, *no*.

"So," I say, "we complete the task, and we get an answer and the captain back?"

Yes, thrums The Knowledge. *Do not fail, or else*.

"What does that mean?" I whisper to Electra. "Else?"

She shrugs. "Something bad."

"All right," I tell The Knowledge. "What do you want us to do?"

Then The Knowledge tells us about the task it wants us to complete. It's something that sounds . . . doable. A metal appendage telescopes out from the wall of light and drops an information chip into Electra's hand.

"Fine," she says. A door opens in the wall, our way out.

Electra casts what seems like a worried glance at the captain and then goes out the door, but I stand there for a moment in the middle of The Knowledge's room of glowing, pulsing light, looking up at the captain, where she's wrapped in a silver web, pinned against the brilliantly bright curved wall.

She gazes down at me for a long moment, then points with her chin at the door. Yes, I should go.

First I lower my voice almost to a whisper, and I know that The Knowledge can sense what I am saying. "Listen," I tell it. "We will complete your task. If you hurt my captain even the tiniest bit, I will shift into the Hunter form, and it will destroy every antenna and dish and ansible on this asteroid. Every eye and every ear, every question and every answer, until you're just a chunk of rock floating through space. Do you understand?"

The light pulses and thrums. Then:

Yes, The Knowledge says.

The task we've been given by The Knowledge is a strange one.

In the same system as its asteroid, orbiting the same weak sun, is a planet. The Knowledge gave Electra a map of a place on this planet called the Vault, where valuable items are stored. In one secure room at the center of the Vault, The Knowledge said, is an object that was stolen from it. It wants the object back.

When I asked The Knowledge what the object is, exactly, it said that I will know it when I see it.

When I asked The Knowledge who stole the object, it said that it didn't know.

The reason it needs me to complete this task is that only a shapeshifter can get past the Vault's defenses to reach the secure center area at its core.

So the plan is that I will go in, collect the object, and then we bring it to the asteroid, we get the captain back, and we get the answer to my question. Then we find the other shapeshifters and . . .

Well, I don't know what happens after that.

It should be easy.

I have this feeling that it won't actually be easy.

It's clear why The Knowledge wanted Electra along. I can't fly the Dart; she can. What this tells me is that The Knowledge knew, even before we arrived on its asteroid, that it was going to kidnap the captain and send me and Electra on a mission to the planet.

It makes me wonder what else it knows, and what we *don't* know.

Electra is ahead of me in the long passageway. When I reach the Dart, she's inside, sitting in the dark, with only the blue lights from the control panel lighting her face. She's frowning down at her hands, on the controls.

I climb in and slide into the other seat.

She doesn't move.

I'm about to open my mouth to say *Let's go*, when she slams her hand down on the panel and the hatch behind us yawns open. She mutters something under her breath, and with a lurch, the Dart lifts from the dock and emerges from the asteroid.

She pushes another button, and the lights inside the Dart come on.

And I realize that we're not alone.

29

The Knowledge's round silvery eye has followed us onto the Dart.

It hovers in front of me.

Watching.

There's nothing we can do about it, I decide. Just in case The Knowledge—back on its asteroid—is letting the captain watch too, I give it a little wave.

Electra is still busy at the controls. Out the front window of the Dart is dark space, and in the distance a brighter star than the rest. That must be the planet on which the Vault is located. It's going to take us a while to get there, I guess.

My stomach growls.

"Is there anything to eat on this ship?" I ask.

Without looking away from the Dart's glowing controls,

Electra points at a latched compartment.

Followed by The Knowledge's eye, I go to it. Except for a few rat droppings, it's empty, not even a scrap of food. I sit on the deck, which is metal, and cold. The inside of the Dart hasn't been made cozy and warm the way the *Hindsight* has been. It's like a small room made of plain, hard plastic and metal, one that happens to be flying through space at high speed toward a distant planet.

Electra pushes one more button, then sits back from the controls. Swiveling her chair, she turns to face me. Seeing The Knowledge's eye hovering near me, she nods, as if she expected it to be there.

Electra seems different. I'm used to seeing her grim and determined, doing exercises to stay strong, fearlessly arguing with the captain, scowling at me.

Right now she seems . . . unhappy. I realize that she never, ever smiles.

"It'll take an hour for the Dart to reach the planet's atmosphere," she tells me.

"I don't think I've ever been on a planet," I realize.

She gives half a shrug.

"What's it like?" I ask.

"I'm not talking to you," she says.

"All right," I say.

She sighs. Her tintacles droop.

I sigh too.

I can ask a question, at least, one that's been bothering me. She doesn't have to answer. "Electra, do you still think that I'm an *it*?"

She frowns.

"I don't know," I go on, "if the Hunter really is . . . if I am . . . a criminal." I pause. "I do know that in the Hunter form, I'm very dangerous."

In a low voice, she says, "You're a lot more dangerous in your human shape."

"What?" I say. "No I'm not." I hold up my human hand. "No sharp claws, no armored skin, no spikes." I bare my blunt human teeth and point to my mouth. "No fangs dripping acid."

"Did the Hunter take over the *Hindsight* and turn everybody on it into an outlaw running from the StarLeague military?" Her voice is bitter. "No. *You* did."

As the captain would say, *Huh*. Electra is right. I must be more devious than I realized. I even fooled myself!

We sit there in silence for a while. Outside the front window, the bright spot that is the planet gets bigger as we get closer to it.

"You'd better show me the map of the Vault," I tell her, "so I can figure out how to get in."

Without speaking, she puts the information chip that The Knowledge gave us into a slot on the control panel and points to a screen on the wall of the Dart; after a moment a map of the Vault comes up.

While I examine the Vault schematic, The Knowledge's eye bobs around the inside of the Dart, looking at everything. My stomach growls again. I turn away from the screen and pick up the conversation where we left off.

"But, I mean," I say, because she didn't really answer me before, "you told the captain that I'm not a *person*. Do you really believe that?" I don't know why it's so important that Electra see me for what I am, but it *is*.

"I don't know what I believe anymore," she says in a low voice.

There's another long silence. A light flashes on the control panel. Electra pushes a button and it stops.

"What was your cadet training like?" I ask.

"Don't try to make me like you," she says. "Because I don't. And I won't."

"You don't have to," I tell her. "I don't expect you to."

She's silent for a while. Outside, the planet is getting bigger. The eye has settled in, hovering at my shoulder. I think it's looking at whatever I look at, and probably watching me at the same time.

"It was hard," Electra says at last.

"What?" I ask.

"My training," she explains. "It began when I was a small child. Education, reeducation, physical endurance, combat training, pilot training, tactics, strategy."

"Did you like it?" I ask.

She pauses to think about it. "Sometimes."

"What can you do?" I ask. "I mean, because of your training?"

She blinks. Then: "Before I was captured, I could have taken over the *Hindsight*. Easily."

"Why didn't you?" I ask.

"Those were not my orders," she tells me.

"Do you always obey orders?" I ask.

"Yes," she says, biting the word and spitting it out.

"Except for when you don't," I say, because there's no chance she's obeying orders right now.

She glares at me. Then she blinks and takes a quick breath, as if she's realized something.

I realize it at the same time. Once I've gone down to the planet to collect this valuable object for The Knowledge, she will be alone on her own Dart ship.

Which means she has a choice to make.

Go or stay.

I have to make sure she knows that it's a real choice. "Electra," I say slowly.

She looks up and meets my eyes. Her hands are clenched into fists. Her tintacles have gone dead black.

"You know the threat that Captain Astra made? That the Hunter would come after you if you try to get away?"

She jerks out a nod.

"I wouldn't ever hurt you," I tell her. "Not even in my Hunter form."

She scowls, but doesn't say anything.

"Are you . . ." I take a shaky breath. "Are you going to be here when I get back?"

Her face is stern. Her tintacles are lying limp on her shoulders. She turns to the Dart controls but doesn't do anything; she just sits there, and she doesn't answer me.

30

I don't remember much from before I was a dog puppy on the station, but I know that I've never seen the curve of a planet looming large in a spaceship window.

From up here, the planet's surface looks smooth, and I can see the thin bubble of its atmosphere. Clouds swirl over most of its surface; below that are glimpses of blue—oceans—and brown—land. We emerge from the planet's shadow, and the weak bluish light of its sun shines into my eyes. The Knowledge's eye is buzzing, as if it's interested in seeing all of it.

"You'd better brace yourself," Electra says in a flat voice. She pushes a button at the controls. "We're about to hit atmosphere."

You already know that space is mostly empty. That's why we call it *space*, right? Right. A ship in outer space cruises along with nothing bumping against it, not even air molecules. Once a ship hits the bubble of air around a planet—the atmosphere—it builds up heat from friction. Not all ships are made to go into atmosphere and down to a planet—the *Hindsight* isn't. That's why it's a cylinder, like a tin can. The Dart is aerodynamic—that is, made to fly through air—and it can go down to a planet.

As we zoom into the atmosphere, the Dart starts to shake, and then the shaking turns to noisy rattling. Out front, the planet gets nearer, taking up the entire window, and flares of heat flash past us. We're falling now, not flying, going faster and faster as the gravity of the planet pulls us in.

After a few loud, rattling minutes, Electra flips a switch and pushes a button, and the Dart's fall turns into a quieter glide. Below us, the surface of the planet is hidden by a thick layer of cloud. She turns toward me. Her face is blank, and I can't tell if she's decided what she's going to do. "Any lower than this, and we'll trigger an alert on the planet. You'll have to get out here."

My heart is beating fast from excitement. "Is the air all right out there? For a human, I mean?"

She checks a reading on the control panel. "It should be fine. You'll fall fast enough that the air will become more breathable fairly quickly. It'll be cold, though."

"That's all right." I'm worried about the captain, of course, and about Electra's choice, and about this strange task that The Knowledge has set for me, but in the meantime, this is going to be *fun*.

The Knowledge's eye bobs over to me. "Are you coming

too?" I ask it. As an answer, it dives down to nestle inside my shirt. It feels cold and smooth against my skin, but after a moment it warms.

Electra fastens a harness around herself and points to the Dart's door. Only clouds are visible now, outside the front window.

"Once the door is open," Electra warns, "you'll be sucked out immediately."

"I'm ready," I say happily, and grin at her, bouncing on my toes. I can't wait to go.

She scowls suddenly and turns away. "The Vault is directly below us," she says. "Goodbye." And she hits a button on the control panel.

As the Dart's outer door opens, I'm sucked out into the howlingly loud, roaring, ice-cold, cloud-damp air. Falling. Flying! *Wheeeeeee!*

I tumble away from the Dart and down, down, down, and then spread my arms and legs wide, and my fall steadies. Air rushes past my ears; my teeth are clenched against the cold. The clouds surround me, a fuzzy blur of white and gray. I'm coated with cloud-wet that quickly freezes, turning to ice that crackles over my skin. I fall and fall and fall, and the air gets warmer and less thin, and I take gasping breaths.

At last I fall out of the clouds into a dazzle of brilliant light.

The planet is spread out below me—so close! It's not smooth anymore, but covered with tall, pointy bumps—mountains!—and green areas that must be forests, and a wide stretch of water that glimmers with sunlight.

"Hold on!" I shout at the eye, the words ripped from my mouth as I fall.

I should have shifted before jumping out of the Dart, but I didn't want to do it in front of Electra, and I wanted to see how my human self would like falling.

I like it enormously, but soft, squishy human me won't like the crashing-into-the-planet's-surface part, so it's time to shift.

The form I choose has powerful leathery wings and a sleek scaled body that is almost as big as the Dart ship. My eyes are very keen; this kind of animal is probably good at spotting its prey from the air. Through those eyes, I immediately see the building that must be the Vault.

You know the word *vault*, don't you? I had to look it up on the screen. A *vault* is "a room or chamber for the safekeeping of valuables."

Sounds pretty simple, doesn't it? You just open the door, step into the vault, get what you want, and go out.

This Vault is *not* simple.

From up high, where I am, the Vault looks like a sphere, but a huge one—almost as big as one of the mountains in the distance. Its outside layer is completely smooth, and made of metal that gleams blue in the setting sun.

Inside, the Vault has layers, one sphere inside another inside another. Think of it as this kind of vegetable called an onion.

There's no easy way in. I'll have to fight my way through every level to reach the smallest center sphere, the Vault's core, where the object is located.

A twitch of my long snaky tail and a flap of my wings, and I arrow toward the Vault, then spiral down to land in a field of vegetation nearby. Grass, I think it's called.

The Knowledge's eye streaks down, landing with a sizzling thud in the grass next to me. Dizzily, it lifts itself out.

I shift back into my human boy form, roll over onto my back, and look up.

The *sky*. It arcs overhead, striped with clouds and far higher than any ship ceiling, any station dock. It is beyond *huge*. And I'm so tiny. I'm used to that, from floating through space in my blob of goo shape, but the sky is different. It presses down on me. I close my eyes and fling my arm over my face and feel certain that I'm about to get squished.

The grass prickles against the skin of my back and legs. I hear the sound of air moving—*wind*, I think it's called?—and the nervous hum of The Knowledge's eye hovering nearby.

Cautiously, I peek out from behind my arm. The sky is still there, a partly cloudy greenish blue, the sun a blue sliver going down behind a faraway mountain.

The Vault looms nearby, a huge metal ball. It gleams dully in the fading sunlight, and its dark shadow covers the grassy hill that I'm lying on.

I sit up. The sky still hasn't crushed me. I guess that means it isn't going to. I shiver as more wind blows over my bare skin. My stomach growls, reminding me that if I'm going to do much more shifting, I will need to eat something. A lot of something, actually. Eight bowls of stew would taste really good right about now.

Whether I have food or not, it's time to complete my mission so I can get my captain back *and* get an answer to my question.

After looking around to see if my clothes happened to fall out of the sky anywhere nearby—they haven't—I start toward the Vault.

31

Shifting into my rat form, I can sense the trail markers that other rats have left outside the Vault. Following the markers, I avoid the alarm sensors, scurrying through grass tunnels and then into a pipe that leads me straight into the building. Along the way I keep my whiskers twitching in case there's any food around—rats will eat *anything*—but there's nothing, really, except grass and then metal and cement.

The Knowledge's eye comes with me, bobbing along behind my slithery rat tail.

The inside of the Vault is a series of concentric spheres, like one ball inside another ball, inside another ball . . . and each level has valuable things in it from different places all over the galaxy.

The object that The Knowledge wants me to bring back to

it is in the very center of the Vault, the innermost, smallest, most secure sphere.

In my rat form, I enter the outer sphere of the Vault, squirming through a drain, emerging into a narrow passageway. The curved walls are made of metal, and there are shelves with objects on them lined up in a long row. Art and handicrafts and tools and weapons, probably organized according to which galactic species made them. I can't see them very well, because rat vision is blurry and sees mostly in darks and lights but not much color, and also I'm low down at floor level. There's a lot of dust in here; it makes my whiskers twitch.

Keeping to the edge of the passageway, I scurry through many twists and turns, places where the passage splits and goes in other directions. The Knowledge's eye follows and my stomach keeps telling me that it's hungry.

There should be a door or a tunnel or something that leads inward, to the next sphere, and I have to find it.

I round a curve and run straight into a shiny, rat-sized metal thing that is trundling along the edge of the wall. It's a robot device; it is sucking up the dust from the corridor floor, and has been scent-marked by a rat—it is not a danger. It stops; a metal antenna swivels, scans me, and scans The Knowledge's eye; then it beeps, changes course, and continues on its way, cleaning as it goes.

Huh. I go on, *scurry-scurry-scurry*, around curves, past a collection of weaponry from somewhere in the outer reaches of the galaxy, down a corridor hung with oil paintings. They are just muddy blurs to my rat eyes, but I'm pretty sure none of them is a picture of *The Lady*. I would know her anywhere. I go on; the eye follows.

Then I stop. The objects on the shelves. I can't see them very well, but I've realized that a sculpture that I just passed seems the same as one I passed earlier.

I patter back to it and gaze up.

It's too blurry. I can't tell.

I'm lost. Rats!

Wait. I'm being stupid. I've been in my human shape for so long that I'm going about this the way a human would—going by sight.

But I'm a rat! And I shouldn't be thinking of this as a storage area—it's a maze.

As it happens, rats are extremely good at figuring out mazes.

Instead of going by sight, I should be paying more attention to the markers left by previous rats that came this way. My nose twitches as I scurry along the passage until—there! An old, faint scent mark. It contains all kinds of information useful to a fellow rat. I follow her trail and it leads me through more twists and turns until I reach an opening in the passage.

I go through it, and the scent marks end, and I realize that if I'm going to make it farther into the Vault, I'm going to have to shift into a different form.

The doorway to the next inner level of the Vault is located at the bottom of a long, narrow shaft. The walls are way too steep and smooth for a rat to climb down.

My blob of goo form could do it, but I don't like to spend too much time in that shape, and I might need it later.

32

My stomach growls.

I know, I tell it. I need to be careful. If I don't find something to eat—and soon—I'll risk running out of energy. I don't have much choice, though. The captain is human and not dangerous like me, and The Knowledge has her, and who knows what it's doing to her. And *Peacemaker* is out there. General Smag may not know exactly where we are, but he has this mysterious ability to find us, so I know I don't have long to complete this mission.

The Knowledge's eye hovers in front of me, buzzing as if it's impatient.

All right. Slowly, to conserve energy, I shift into the form of a gekkonid, an amphibious being that has five bulbous toes at the end of each of its four legs; each toe is covered with tiny hairs that make the toes super grippy and able to stick to almost any surface. Most gekkonids live on space stations and work as janitors who clean walls and ceilings.

In my gekkonid form, I skitter straight down the wall, followed by The Knowledge's eye, to the round door at the bottom of the shaft.

When I get there, I realize that I'm going to have to shift again. Gekkonid toes are very good at clinging to walls, but not so good at opening latches.

I shift into my human form because hands with opposable thumbs are good at opening tricky things, go through, and immediately have to shift into a crystal spider form that comes from an airless ice planet and is not affected by the cold. This level of the Vault is frozen, with shards of light glittering from every sharp surface. Using the spider's eight legs, I make my way past elaborate sculptures made of frozen water with steaming liquid nitrogen waterfalls, towering icicles, elaborate laceworks of ice crystals.

I make it through to the next door. Hah! Take that, frozen ice sphere!

With an effort, I shift out of the crystal spider form and into the form of tiny insectoids with a collective mind. They squeeze through the narrow crack that is the next door, and into the next sphere. This one has no gravity, and I have to shift again into a creature that can travel through it. And then to the next level, which is for methane breathers, so I have to shift again. And then to the next. And the next.

All the while I'm aware of the time passing, General Smag getting closer, the captain waiting and maybe in danger.

And I'm getting hungrier.

The next shift, into a scaled, cold-blooded being that can breathe water, is much harder. I make it through that level and realize that at some point I lost The Knowledge's eye. I am so hungry that the hunger is all I can think about. It doesn't just growl, it roars.

After the water sphere, my fish form flops onto a hard surface for a moment, and then I shift, slowly, into my human form. I lie there, dripping wet and panting. *Stew*, I think. *Noodles. Protein bars. More stew.*

Slowly, I sit up.

And I realize that I have a problem.

The sphere I'm in is noticeably smaller than the rest. That means I am close to the center of the Vault, its core. I am about to find the object that The Knowledge sent me here for. This is good.

The problem is that I have to not only find the object, but bring it back out again, and that means shifting through level after level until I'm outside the Vault.

"All right," I whisper, and I'm alarmed at how shaky my voice sounds.

I'll just deal with the next steps when I come to them. I can't think about the captain or about other shapeshifters or about Electra's choice and whether she'll be waiting for me when I get out of the Vault. I just have to get the object.

Slowly, I get to my knees and then totter to my feet. My head spins, and I put a hand back against the wall to steady myself. I'm on a small ledge that runs around the inside of the sphere. The metal walls curve in above and below me. There's no light except from a round platform that floats at the very center of the sphere. Something is resting on it, and it is glowing.

That must be it. The object at the very center of the Vault that I am supposed to bring back to the asteroid. The Knowledge said I would know it when I saw it.

I squint. The object is . . .

. . . is it a bowl of stew?

I think it is. With wisps of steam coming off it. And a spoon, which I don't think I'm even going to bother with. Oh, I can almost smell the protein-cubey and brown-sauce goodness. *GO*, my stomach roars at me.

I realize that I have no way of getting over to it except by shifting into a creature that can fly—and then a narrow bridge unfolds from the ledge that I'm standing on.

"Come on, Trouble," I tell myself.

Taking a steadying breath, I start across the bridge. With each step I take toward the bowl of stew, the bridge falls away behind me. There's no way back—except by shifting.

Halfway across I stop to rest, panting, feeling like I'm carrying an entire spaceship on my shoulders. For one gasping breath I have time to think that I might be making a big mistake, and then the bridge below my feet starts to crumble away and

I have to go forward again. Stumbling, I make it the rest of the way across, to the center of the sphere.

It's a circular metal platform just a little wider than I am tall. Around its edges is a faint glow.

There is nothing on it. No bowl of delicious stew. Not even a scrap of a drip of sauce or a lingering aroma.

Wait. What?

Under my feet, the last remaining section of bridge gives a tingle and then falls away.

Using the last of my strength, I scramble onto the platform to keep from falling. The moment I touch the platform's surface, a globe of light snaps into place, enclosing me in a small spherical room.

And I realize that I've just stepped into a trap.

33

Immediately I try to jab my hand through the wall of light, and it gives me a shock, just like the one I got from the restraining cuff in the mess-room of the *Hindsight*. The shock leaves me sprawled on the round platform, staring up at the dome of light overhead. The platform is ice-cold, and I start to shiver.

I'm too hungry to move. My stomach isn't even bothering to growl anymore; it's become a gaping black hole inside me.

I cannot *believe* how stupid I am, walking right into this trap. The Knowledge even gave us a hint. It told us that it didn't know who stole the object it was sending me to find. But it's The Knowledge—it knows everything! I should have realized that it was tricking us.

The Hunter could escape from here, I find myself thinking.

If I could shift into the Hunter, which I can't, because I'm completely out of energy.

I could manage to shift into my blob of goo form. It's the shape that's easiest. The blob of goo might even be able to escape from this round prison made of light. But it would take a long time—because I'm so drained of energy, I'd have to squeeze out slowly, molecule by molecule, and I'd run a big risk of forgetting the captain and Reetha and the *Hindsight* and Electra and everything.

I won't do it.

There's a faint buzzing sound, and a small door opens in the wall of light that surrounds me.

The Knowledge's eye pops out of the door and hovers nearby.

"Hello," I croak at it.

The eye buzzes, which I guess means *hello*.

Then I speak directly to The Knowledge, because I know it is listening, and that it is the only one clever enough to set a trap like this. "Did you capture me for the StarLeague?" I ask. "Is General Smag coming to get me?"

The eye buzzes again, and this time The Knowledge's deep, thrumming voice emerges from it. *No. The StarLeague cannot find you here. You are being helped. You are mine.*

Oh no. The Knowledge doesn't just collect information, it collects things, and it stores them in the Vault. Now it has collected me. That means I won't be able to rescue the captain or find the shapeshifters or go back to the *Hindsight*. . . .

The eye drifts closer, examining me. I know I must look terrible, splatted on the floor, completely out of energy.

"My captain will come and get me out of here," I whisper.

Captain Astra will be returned to her ship and it will depart. The StarLeague cadet will return to her master. You will stay here, where you are safe.

Its words make me shiver all over. I want to be safe, but not *this* kind of safe. "No," I tell it. "You're wrong. The *Hindsight* won't leave without me."

No one is coming for you, The Knowledge says, and it sounds certain.

So certain. What if it is right?

Maybe I caused too much trouble this time. I made a stupid mistake. Maybe Captain Astra isn't coming for me after all.

At the thought, tears leak out of the corners of my eyes, and I'm too weak to lift a hand to brush them away.

Even if I manage to escape, will the *Hindsight* already be gone? And Electra, too?

The eye bobs closer, and its buzz turns into more of a hum. It's almost comforting.

"Listen," I say to it, and my voice is a whisper that I can barely hear over the roaring of my hunger. "If you're keeping me here, you'll have to give me something to eat." Or I will die. And soon.

As an answer, a thin metal appendage emerges from the

wall of light. I feel a needle prick against the skin of my arm, and then—nothing.

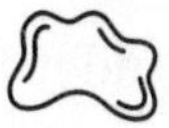

When I wake up, I'm lying in the middle of the platform. I'm wearing clothes, a shirt and pants made out of a plain white material. The air in my prison is warmer. And . . . I'm not *quite* as hungry. I lever myself into a sitting position and push up the sleeve of my shirt. There's the mark of a needle on the skin at the inside of my elbow.

The Knowledge has figured out a way to give me enough energy to keep me alive without feeding me enough so that I can shift and escape from its prison.

I wrap my arms around my legs and rest my chin on my knees.

I'm still shivering. But not from the cold.

Does your species do this thing called *dreaming*?

It's something humans do. When they are asleep, they see stories inside their heads. I know, it's weird, but that's humans for you. The stories can be snippets of things that happened, or imagined things, but while the human is asleep and dreaming them, they seem like they're really *real*.

While I was unconscious, or sleeping, I had my very first dream ever.

It was not a good dream.

The dream started out here, in The Knowledge's round white quiet trap at the center of its Vault. And then it changed. It became a different, bigger room—a prison—with metal instruments, gleaming devices, blindingly white walls, people in white coats.

And me, in the middle of it all, alone and ravenously hungry.

Me, being watched all the time.

Trying to escape. Struggling, fighting, resisting.

Being forced to take shape after shape after shape until I didn't know who I was, or *what* I was.

Until I woke up, shaking and shivering and scared.

I don't think that shiny white room was a dream place. I think it was real. It was my *before.*

It was the place I escaped from before I ended up at that station in the shape of a dog puppy. It must be the prison. What did I *do* that I was put into such an awful place?

The Knowledge's eye bobs closer. In its curved, reflective surface I see my face, pale, thinner than it was before, dark circles under my eyes.

I frown, and my reflected face looks like Electra's: grim, determined. I know what Electra would do in this situation. She would fight.

"You're wrong about Captain Astra," I tell the eye.

I am never wrong, The Knowledge intones.

"Yes you are," I insist.

Your tiny brain cannot encompass what The Knowledge knows, it says.

"Your giant galactic brain doesn't know anything about humans," I say, my voice shaking, "if you think my captain will leave me here. Because she won't."

Carefully, I get to my feet. I am *not* going back to that prison, the one I dreamed about, and I'm not staying in this prison either.

For a moment I study the glowing globe of light that surrounds me. Taking a deep breath, I try to step through it. There's a crackle and a flash, and the shock crashes through me, and a second later I'm flat on my back, trying to catch my breath.

The Knowledge's eye buzzes around me, concerned.

As soon as I can manage it, I climb back to my feet. I'm trembling so hard, I can barely stand.

The prison dream.

Captain. Other shapeshifters.

Must escape.

A metal appendage zips out from the wall; I lurch away from its grabbing claws, and then duck as another appendage tipped with a needle comes after me.

Gritting my teeth, clenching my fists, I fling myself at the wall again.

This time the shock sends me down into the darkness.

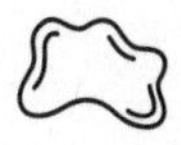

I stay in the dark for a long time.

There are no stars. There's no singing.

A long, long time. It's like being in my blob of goo form, floating through empty space.

Captain Astra, I remind myself. *The* Hindsight. *The crew. Other shapeshifters. Safety. Home.*

Then, in the far distance, I hear other noises.

A rumble. And then, nearer, an echoing *boom* and the sound of something cracking open. The platform under me shivers.

And I feel a hand on my shoulder.

It jerks me out of the drifting darkness. I open my eyes, squinting against the light.

It's Electra, crouched on the platform next to me. Wind is rushing past her. She has a smear of grease across her cheek, her tintacles are waving wildly, and she's wearing her most determined look.

"E-Electra?" I croak, blinking up at her. "What are you doing here?"

"Come on, Trouble with a *T*," she says, and her green eyes gleam with excitement. "We're getting you out of here."

34

"Here," Electra says, and pulls five protein bars out of a pocket in her coverall and drops them onto my chest.

Food! I manage to sit up.

She is crouched beside me, on the alert, with a weapon drawn and ready. She has some sort of sword strapped across her back, and knives and a stun weapon at her belt. The bubble of light that had imprisoned me has disappeared, and so has The Knowledge's eye; we're at the center of the Vault, the platform an island in the darkness. There's a crack in the curved wall, and water from the next level is leaking in. In the distance, alarms are going off and there's a low rumbling sound and I can smell smoke. Did *Electra* do all this?

"The Knowledge will send more defenses after us," she says, scanning the area.

I fumble with a protein bar. My hands are shaking so much, I can't even open it. It's very frustrating!

Without dropping her guard, Electra reaches over, rips open a bar, and shoves it back into my hands. "Eat fast," she orders.

"How did you—" I start, with my mouth full of protein bar. I'm so glad she's here!

"Shut up," she interrupts as she whirls, aiming her laser weapon at a swarm of metal stun-darts that have erupted from a door in the curved wall of the larger sphere. Four of them explode into flowers of fire; two more keep coming, arrowing toward us.

Smoothly, Electra draws the sword from its sheath at her back and with a single slice cuts both darts out of the air.

She spares me a glance. "Are you eating, T?"

No, I was watching. Quickly, I finish the first protein bar. My hands are steadier, so I don't have any trouble opening the second. "Where did you get all those weapons?" I ask through my next mouthful.

"Here," she says.

"But—" I start to say.

"Not now," she orders. She taps a band on her wrist and speaks into it. "Yes, I've got him, Reetha." She pauses and listens to something. Then: "Relax. He's fine." She glances over at me. "You're fine, right?"

I nod and stuff another bar into my mouth. Better every second!

"Yes," she is saying into the band. "He needs another minute, and then we'll start." She taps the band again and says to me, "You've got about thirty seconds and we have to move. Can you shift?"

I climb to my feet, devouring the fourth protein bar. "Yep. What do you mean, that you got the weapons *here*?"

"The Knowledge gave us the schematics to this place, right? Stupid of it. The outer level included a collection of weaponry." She slides the sword back into its sheath. "When I realized you were having problems down here, I took the Dart back to the *Hindsight*, got you some food, came back here, and fired a targeted blast from the Dart that penetrated the Vault."

She makes it sound like a report, and she makes it sound easy, but I don't think it was.

There's a deep rumble from the Vault, and another alarm starts blaring, louder than before.

Ignoring it, Electra goes on, "Then I broke into the outer level of the Vault, where I found the rest of the weapons that I needed, and fought my way into its center, which is where I figured you'd be."

Electra, I realize, is extremely good at what she does.

"How did you know—" I begin, because I want to ask her how she knew that I was here, exactly, and that I needed help, but she holds up a hand.

"Later. For now we have to get out of here. Ready to shift?"

Five protein bars can't put me back at full strength, but

they're enough. Clearly I am our way out. Quickly, I move to the edge of the platform and shift into my big, leather-winged, snake-tailed, sleek-bodied self.

"That'll do," Electra says, and without even a moment of hesitation she climbs onto my back. "Follow the trail of the blast—we're going out the same way I came in."

As she speaks, the Vault sends another attack at us.

"Go!" Electra shouts, and I spread my wings wide and launch myself from the platform.

Pursued by a flock of telescoping robot arms with needles at their tips, I bank; at the same time, Electra fires her weapon. "Up!" she orders, and I crank my wings and we shoot upward. My keen eyes spot the ragged tunnel that Electra had blasted through all the layers of the Vault, with a window of light on its other end—sunlight. This is our way out. As Electra fires her weapon behind us, I zoom through the tunnel, through one layer after another, banking around attacking crystal spiders, swooshing around a waterfall of liquid nitrogen, holding my breath through a puff of methane, until I see sunlight directly ahead. A mighty flap of my wings, and I aim myself toward it.

A second later we shoot out into the air, under the sky—free.

Outside the Vault, I land, Electra hops to the ground, and I shift back into my human boy shape again. The Dart is waiting, sitting on a burned circle of grass where it must have landed. The blue sun is shining dimly behind a layer of clouds. Nearby, the Vault is a huge broken metal egg with smoke streaming from its cracks and water gushing from other cracks. I hope all the rats in there are all right. They probably are—they're always the first to know when trouble is around.

"Hurry," Electra says, putting her weapon away and scanning the area. "Landing the Dart set off alarms, and I've been here too long already."

The shifting drained my energy again, but I manage to stagger onto the Dart and into a seat . . .

. . . when I realize that The Knowledge's eye has caught up to us and followed me in.

"Electra!" I exclaim, pointing at it.

She turns from the controls. Her eyes narrow. "We're coming for you," she threatens The Knowledge, speaking directly to the eye.

It cowers, then zips around to hide behind me.

"You're mistaken," I tell it over my bare shoulder, "if you think I'm going to protect you."

The eye buzzes unhappily.

Electra swivels back to the controls. "Hold on," she snaps. "This is going to be messy."

35

By *messy*, Electra means completely, terrify-ingly bumpy, but we lift off and claw our way through the atmosphere, and at last the Dart comes out into the smooth darkness of space. I can almost see why the captain likes it better out here.

Electra pushes a few buttons and then leans back in her chair, releasing a deep, relieved breath. "*Hindsight* is holding its position at the asteroid," she says. "We need to hurry, but it's still going to be another hour before we arrive." She swivels her chair. Seeing me, she shakes her head. "There are clothes for you over there." She points.

On unsteady feet I go to the compartment and find a coverall and a colorful sweater and foot coverings, which I put on, and another supply of protein bars, which I start eating at once, sitting on the floor with my back against a wall.

Electra is busy inspecting each of her weapons before laying them out on the control panel.

"The captain," I say through a mouthful of food, because I'm worried about Captain Astra. The Knowledge has her, she could be in danger, and we might be too late to save her. I am feeling very *human* about the situation.

Electra glances at me. "I know." She holds the sword at arm's length, checking the edge of its blade, and then slides it into its sheath. "We'll get her back."

And because it's Electra saying that, I believe her, and the worry lifts a little.

"How did you know I was in trouble?" I ask.

"You're always in trouble," she answers without looking at me.

Did she just make a joke? She's not smiling. Maybe not.

Electra sets down the laser weapon. After a moment she gets out of her chair and sits on the floor, opposite me.

I toss her a protein bar, just in case she's hungry.

She tosses it back. "Let me ask you this, T. You escaped from a StarLeague prison. How did General Smag know you were on the station?"

I blink. "I don't know."

She nods grimly as if she expected my answer. "And how did the *Peacemaker* keep tracking the *Hindsight*, even though Captain Astra's ship had the stealth-box and made evasive maneuvers, and I wasn't signaling him?"

"I don't know," I say again. "The captain didn't know either."

"Well, I've been thinking about that, and about something The Knowledge said," she goes on. "Do you remember?"

The Knowledge said a lot of things. I shake my head, *no*.

"It said that when you shift, you release a unique kind of energy. Once I knew to look for it, the Dart sensors were picking it up. From orbit. Do you see what I'm saying here?"

My mouth is full of protein bar, but I stop chewing and stare at her.

She nods. "If this Dart could detect your shifting energy, so could the *Peacemaker*. General Smag knows exactly where you are because you were shifting over and over again while you were in the Vault. That's how he tracked you to the station, too."

This gives me a cold, creepy feeling.

All along I've thought that shapeshifting was helping me to escape.

And it was really helping General Smag to pursue me.

Electra goes on. "After you left, I was tracking your shifter energy. You hadn't been gone for very long when the numbers started to go down." She frowns at me. "You were getting weaker."

"I was very hungry," I tell her, finishing yet another protein bar.

"Why didn't you say something before you left?" she asks, a note of exasperation in her voice.

"I did!" I protest. "I asked if there was any food on the Dart."

"You must have known that you were going to run out of energy," she challenges.

"I wasn't sure," I tell her. "And I had to do what The Knowledge said so I could get the captain back and find out about the shapeshifters."

"But why didn't you tell me!" She seems really angry now.

I'm a little angry too. "Because I thought you didn't like me." I think back over our conversation. "You *told* me you didn't like me. You never wanted to talk to me. You called me *it* and *thing*!"

We both glare at each other.

The Knowledge's eye peeks out from behind one of the seats, and then ducks away again to hide.

Electra sighs and slumps against the wall. "You're right."

I realize suddenly that she's changed her mind about me, but it's more than that. "Electra, why did you rescue me?" I ask.

"Because you're dangerous," she answers.

I wait.

"Because . . ." she says. She looks unhappy again. "Do you remember the captain's test? You passed because you offered to give yourself up to save the ship. But I failed, remember?"

I nod, *yes*.

"I failed because I kept insisting that you were not a person. I've been thinking a lot about that." After a moment she goes on, and her voice gets very quiet. "At that moment, T, you were a better person than I was."

Slowly, I get up and go over to sit down next to her.

Electra will never, ever cry, but I know she feels the misery water inside her. I pat her arm. "It might not matter," I tell her, "but I liked you almost from the moment you came onto the ship."

"Of course you did, T," she says, that bitterness in her voice again. "That's why you're so dangerous."

We sit quietly for a moment. I feel jittery with the need to hurry, to get the captain and get back to the *Hindsight* so we can escape before General Smag and the *Peacemaker* arrive, because I *know* they are coming with all speed. But the Dart can't go any faster, and we have another half an hour before we get to the asteroid.

"Electra?" I ask, because she really hasn't answered my question.

She sniffs. "What," she says, sounding a little cross. Her tintacles are faintly golden colored, and lying limp on her shoulders as if they are tired.

"Why didn't you leave? General Smag is coming with the *Peacemaker*," I say. "You could have shown him right where I was. You would have been a hero."

She's quiet for a second. "Remember when Amby told us about their home planet and their parental units and their pod-siblings and the nest they grew up in?"

I nod.

"I never had that." She takes a shaky breath. "The

StarLeague identified me as a good candidate to be a cadet. They took me away from my mother when I was a baby."

"What's a baby?" I ask.

She casts me an annoyed glance. "It's when humanoids are small and young, right after they've been born."

I have *no* idea what she's talking about.

She brings up a picture on the Dart's screen and shows me.

Ohhhh. I've seen pictures of babies before. There were lots of pictures in the art of Earth, second era, of ladies holding babies on their laps. I'd thought they were some kind of pet. But no! They were young humans.

And then . . . they change, and their heads get smaller, their arms and legs get longer, and they can walk around and talk. They grow up. To be kids! Like me, and like Electra. And then adults, like Captain Astra.

All kids, I realize, are shapeshifters!

Then I try to imagine Electra as a baby. I bet she was cute. "Do you remember your home?" I ask her.

"Not really," she answers. "Only that, when the StarLeague came to take me away, my mother cried."

Crying. I know about that now. It's when you fill up with sadness until it spills out your eyes.

"That's all I remember," Electra says sadly. "My mother with tears running down her face, and her tintacles all pale and drooping. After that I never saw her again."

36

Now I know why Electra decided to stop being a cadet. Because the StarLeague took away her family and her home.

That is a very good reason.

"*No,*" Electra is saying into her wristband communication device. "Reetha, just let me and Trouble get the captain back from The Knowledge. You stay on the ship."

The asteroid, still bristling with antennae, is looming large in the Dart's forward window. Beyond it is the dented tin can that is the *Hindsight*.

I'm on my feet, ready to go. The Knowledge's eye hovers next to me.

"General Smag has almost certainly detected Trouble's shifting energy. He is probably on his way to the Vault," Electra says to Reetha. "So we have a little time until he figures out that Trouble isn't there anymore. Make sure the ship is ready to go to pulse engines and turn on the stealth-box as soon as we get back with the captain." She pauses. "Yes, we'll hurry." She says a few more words to Reetha, and then pushes a button on the control panel. We slow, and ease toward the asteroid's dock.

As we approach, it opens. The Knowledge is letting us in.

Electra, fully armed again, comes to stand next to me by the outer hatch. "Ready?" she asks, with a glance at the eye.

"Yes," I say. I've had enough to eat; I'm ready.

"Stay back," she advises. "Once we've got the captain, you're going to shift into the Hunter and we're going to destroy The Knowledge."

"Wait." I grab her sleeve. "No. We can't do that."

"Why not?" Electra asks, jerking her arm away from me. "The Knowledge knew you were coming, lured you into its prison-Vault-thing, and trapped you there. Seriously, T, give me one reason why I shouldn't blast it to pieces."

At my shoulder, the eye buzzes with alarm. "It's all right," I tell it. I'm not happy with The Knowledge for kidnapping the captain and for trying to lock me in its prison, but it really did think it was keeping me safe, and I'm pretty sure it doesn't intend to hurt the captain, and . . . there's another reason.

"I think it's lonely," I tell Electra.

She stares at me. *"Lonely?"*

"It's the only one of its kind," I tell her. "It's like I was before

I found the captain and Reetha and the *Hindsight*." Then I add, "And you."

Electra takes a breath. Then another. "Lonely," she mutters under her breath. Then she checks one of the weapons at her belt, looks up at the ceiling, and then back at me. "All right," she agrees at last. "We won't blast it."

"Good." I bounce on my toes, ready to go.

The Dart docks, and we step out into the dark tunnel. The light of The Knowledge's room gleams in the distance.

Without speaking, Electra and I pace toward it. The light grows brilliantly bright, and we step into it. I look around quickly, but the captain is not there.

As before, the curved walls are pulsing with a low thrum. We stand on the flat place, and we wait. I feel jittery. The eye hovers at my shoulder.

Greetings, says The Knowledge, sounding weirdly calm.

The bone-deep rumble of its voice has the same effect it did before. It makes my skin bumpy and my hair prickly.

Beside me, Electra looks determined and completely in control. "We've come for the captain of the *Hindsight*," she says.

Thrum, thrum, thrum.

"Please," I add. Always good to be polite with hyperintelligent, powerful beings.

Then, across the room from us, my captain steps half out of the light, blinking. She looks around, catches sight of me and Electra, and nods.

Seeing her, I feel a hugely human reaction of relief.

"And now," Electra says firmly to The Knowledge, "you will give us the information about shapeshifters." She raises her voice. "Unless, of course, you want to argue with us about it." She puts her hand threateningly on one of the weapons at her belt.

At my shoulder, the eye buzzes in alarm.

The light pulses. *There will be no arguing,* The Knowledge intones. *We are not enemies.*

Suddenly, from behind me, one of The Knowledge's telescopic arms shoots out of the wall of light. I flinch away from it.

"Should I blast it?" Electra hisses.

The Knowledge only wants to help, it says. The arm snakes closer.

"I'm going to blast it," Electra threatens.

"No!" I blurt out. "It's not going to hurt us. It's not our enemy."

I hold out my hand, and the robotic arm drops a small square information chip into my palm.

The answer to your question, The Knowledge says. *The location of the shapeshifters.*

I close my hand around the chip. "Thank you," I say.

Across the room, Captain Astra pulls herself farther out of the light and starts toward us. I'm so, so glad to see her. I don't know what humans do in this kind of situation.

The captain gets halfway across the room, and then she stops and opens her arms. "Come here," she says.

I step closer, and the captain comes to meet me, and wraps

her arms around me. I feel her kiss the top of my head. "You're all right?" she asks.

"Yes," I say. "Are *you* all right?"

I hear her mutter something, but I can't quite make out the words. She lets me go, and I step away.

The captain must see the confusion on my face, because she smiles. "That was a hug, Trouble. It means I'm glad to see you."

"I am *extremely* glad to see you," I tell her.

"I'll bet," Captain Astra says. "Now let's get out of here."

The Knowledge thrums, and then speaks. *You must hurry,* it says in its deep voice. *This message arrived only a short time ago.*

And then a section of the curved wall goes dim, and in place of the light, a recording of a giant General Smag appears. The sight of his bulbous forehead and jutting chin and his beady black eyes looming over our heads makes me shiver.

"*Knowledge unit,*" he says in his commanding voice. "*We have detected activity on the planet indicating that a dangerous escaped criminal is in the vicinity, and it must be recaptured. You are in great danger. My ship will arrive at the planet in less than one hour. Close your dock and admit no one to your asteroid.*" The screen goes dark again, and then light.

Another human reaction hits me—fear. I remember the dream I had when I was in the Vault, the dream about the terrible prison with the hunger, and the bright lights and shiny metal, and the fear, and how it felt so *real.* General Smag wants to put me back in that place.

"Come on," Electra says, and heads for the door, followed by the captain.

I'm about to step out, following them, when the eye buzzes up to me and, at the same time, The Knowledge says my name.

Trouble, it booms.

I pause in the doorway. Electra and the captain are ahead, running down the passageway toward the Dart.

"I don't have time to talk to you," I tell The Knowledge.

Wait, it says. *There is information. Knowledge. You will find it where you are going.*

"Information about what?" I ask. "Shapeshifters?"

Knowledge about The Knowledge, it answers. *Will you allow an eye to accompany you*?

Ohhhh. The eye bobs up to me, level with my face. I gaze into it.

I think of all the times people have looked at me and seen—well, I don't know what they see. The dog puppy, the human boy, the Hunter. And I've wondered if they see *me.*

I don't see me, reflected in The Knowledge's eye. I see something else.

The Knowledge has questions about itself, just like I have questions about who I am and what I'm for.

"Yes," I tell it. "Your eye can come with me. And I hope it finds out what you need to know."

The eye hums.

Thank you, The Knowledge says politely.

37

The second the outer hatch is closed and we step off the Dart and onto the *Hindsight*, the captain is running down the corridor, shouting for Shkkka and for Amby. She'll get them to switch on the stealth-box so we can stay hidden from the *Peacemaker*—for now and as long as I don't shapeshift.

The Knowledge's eye has come with us. It's here to watch everything and keep The Knowledge informed. With it bobbing behind me, I follow Electra to the mess-room. Reetha is there, waiting.

"Hello," I say, and give half a wave. Somehow I think *hug* is not something you do with lizardians.

Reetha says nothing, just takes a long look at me with her glittering golden eyes.

"See?" Electra says to her. "I told you he was fine."

Reetha ignores that, and then she turns and stalks out of the room.

One of these days I should shift into a lizardian so I can better understand how Reetha thinks.

But not now. I flop down onto the couch, feeling suddenly and overwhelmingly tired. And *safe*. The mess-room is colorful, shabby, and warm, and there's nowhere else in the galaxy I'd rather be.

Electra starts taking off her weapons and setting them on the table. The eye is floating around the room, looking at everything.

My stomach growls. I peel myself off the couch and go into the galley, where I open a cupboard. The first thing I see is a packet of stew.

For a flash I'm back in the center of the Vault, looking across a dark space at a glowing bowl of stew . . . that isn't really there. My stomach lurches. Not stew. I reach for three packets of noodles instead, and make myself a giant bowl of them, with bright orange cheese powder. I take the bowl to the table, push aside one of Electra's knives and a laser weapon, and dig in.

The captain comes in looking satisfied. The stealth-box must be working. "Good, you're eating," she says to me, and heads for the galley, where she gets herself a cup of kaff.

I notice that Electra is standing at attention.

The captain comes out of the galley. "At ease, Cadet," she says dryly.

Electra relaxes, but not much.

Captain Astra takes a sip of kaff, looking at me over the rim of her cup. "I was very annoyed with you," she says, "for falling into The Knowledge's trap."

"There was stew," I say.

"*Stew?*" Electra puts in. "You were trapped by *stew*?"

I nod. "I was extremely hungry." Then I explain: "But it wasn't really stew after all."

"T, you idiot," Electra says.

The captain, watching us, has a strange half smile on her face. "So, Electra," she drawls.

Electra stiffens again.

"The Knowledge," the captain goes on, "let me watch the entire Vault fiasco through its eye. As far as I could see, it was mostly Trouble getting into trouble and you rescuing him." She cocks an eyebrow. "Does that sound about right?"

"Yes," Electra bites out.

"Why?" is all the captain asks.

Electra looks down at the floor.

I know her; I know what she's feeling. "Because she didn't pass your test," I tell the captain. "That's why."

"Huh," Captain Astra says.

"That's not the only reason," Electra says. Her tintacles have turned golden for sadness. "When I was small, the StarLeague took me away from my home and my family so they could train me to become a Dart pilot."

The captain nods as if she's not surprised. "The StarLeague does that."

"They shouldn't," Electra says firmly, as if she's just realized this. "It's wrong."

"Yeah," the captain agrees. "It is." She pulls out a chair to sit at the table. "Now, thanks to the stealth-box, we're hidden in a space-pocket, so we should be safe from the general's pursuit for a while. Let's see where we have to go to find the other shapeshifters." I hand her the information chip that The Knowledge gave me. The remote is on the table; she inserts the chip. The captain and Electra lean closer, watching as information starts appearing on the screen, bright numbers and star charts and coordinates, and then a big schematic. The eye hovers just behind them.

I don't start eating again. We're about to find out where the other shapeshifters are. I wonder if it will be what I imagined. Maybe it'll be a planet with others like me, a place that I came from. Or maybe . . .

Electra and the captain go very still. They are both staring at a star chart that is splayed across the screen. Numbers float under it, and words that I can't read from where I am sitting.

"It must be," the captain says.

"It can't be," Electra says.

The captain glances at me. "Trouble, what do you remember about the prison you were in?"

I blink at the unexpected question. "Nothing," I tell her.

Except for the terrible dream I had about it, with the fear and the hunger and the metal and the white lights. "The blob of goo form can't store memories for very long."

The captain rubs her eyes. "This is bad."

I don't quite understand what she's talking about.

Seeing my confusion, she says, "The Knowledge gave us the information about where to find the other shapeshifters. They're in a prison. It's just . . ." She trails off.

"Where?" I ask. "Where's the prison? Where are they?"

"I'm sorry, kiddo," the captain says softly. "The prison is on board the *Peacemaker*."

Oh.

Oh *no*.

The other shapeshifters are in a prison on General Smag's ship.

The same prison I must have escaped from.

Electra is peering more closely at the screen. "Wait." With a shaking finger, she uses the remote to scroll past some numbers and then freezes the display on a map of a ship. "Look at these schematics." Electra swallows. "It's on the *Peacemaker*, but it's not— T, the place you escaped from is not a prison. It's a high-security weapons laboratory."

I don't get it. "Why would I be there?"

"*Weapons* lab," Electra repeats, and gazes across the table at me. "A place where new weapons are developed. It's where you came from."

As I realize what this means, I get a sudden lurching, empty feeling, like when I was floating in the deepest, coldest, most airless regions of space. There's no *home*. There's no family of shapeshifters waiting for me.

I really am a thing.

I was made in a lab.

To be a weapon.

38

I think I've known all along that I am a weapon.

When anyone looks into my eyes, that's what they should see: a thing that was made for hunting and for killing. They don't see a person, they see an *it.*

"He will never agree," Electra is saying.

The captain answers, but I can't hear her above the whirling of my thoughts.

There are other shapeshifters, like me. Other made weapons. Except they haven't escaped from the lab on the *Peacemaker*, as I did.

From the time I arrived at the station and took the shape of a dog puppy, I knew that I was running away from something. I always knew it was something awful.

The dream I had, with the white walls and the hunger and the desperate resistance. It wasn't a prison; it was a *lab*.

And now I'm going to have to go back to it. Because if there are shapeshifters still in that lab, they are alone and frightened, and I have to get them out.

I realize that I am standing in the middle of the mess-room, and the Hunter is stirring. A blink, and I see that Electra and the captain are still at the table. The eye has disappeared; it's probably hiding. Reetha has come in too, and waits by the door with her arms folded. The captain has her head in her hands, and Electra looks as bleak as I've ever seen her.

The captain looks up. "Trouble, we'll head for the Altarian system. The Free Farmers will take you and hide you from the StarLeague. And Electra, too. You'll both be safe there."

Electra is shaking her head.

When I speak, my voice sounds hoarse, as if I've been shouting. "No," I rasp. I pace two steps away, and then two steps back to the middle of the room. "I have to get the other shapeshifters out of that place."

"Told you," Electra says.

"Shut up," the captain snarls at her.

"I have to get them out of that lab," I repeat.

"Trouble, you can*not*," the captain says, getting to her feet. "You should run as far away from there as you can."

I turn to face her. "No."

"I will *not* hand you over to that StarLeague general." She bangs a hand on the table. "That's what this would amount to. I won't do it."

I don't know what my face looks like, but she flinches. "If you won't take me to the *Peacemaker*," I say in my raspy voice, "I'll go by myself." I whirl and head for the door, the one that opens onto the corridor that leads to the airlock.

Reetha gets there ahead of me. She plants herself in front of the door, her arms still folded and her face as blank as it always is.

"Get out of my way," I warn. There is a thing that I have to do, and nobody is going to stop me from doing it.

Reetha just stands there. A blink and I will shift into the Hunter, and I will fight my way out.

"Stop it!" It's Electra. Swiftly, she crosses the room to me and grips the front of my sweater, holding me in place when I try to pull away. "Listen, T. Just listen. You know why I decided to help you, instead of turning you in? You were on the planet, trapped in the Vault, and I was waiting in the Dart, and I had to decide. I could have alerted General Smag, and he would have been the one to take you out of The Knowledge's trap." She pulls me closer. "Why didn't I?"

"Because the StarLeague took you from your family when you were a baby," I say.

"That's right," Electra says. "You've seen what I can do; you know how dangerous I am. I was made by the StarLeague, just like you were." She lets go of my sweater and puts her hands on my shoulders. "We are weapons, T. But we are people, too."

I consider it. If we are people, then we can't be *used* by somebody else. We get to decide. "I am a weapon," I tell her, "that is for rescuing shapeshifters."

"*Yes*," she says fiercely. "So am I." Electra glances over her shoulder at Reetha. "Are you in?"

"Yes," Reetha answers immediately.

I turn to the captain, because we can't do anything unless she agrees to help.

Before I can speak, Reetha points at her with a claw. "Confess," she orders.

The captain blinks. "Maybe now isn't the—"

"*Confess*," Reetha insists.

"Yes. Well." The captain scrubs a hand through her tightly curled hair. "Trouble, you know that we do a bit of smuggling on this ship."

"Yes," I say, remembering our conversation about that.

"I *knew* it," Electra whispers beside me.

"Right, well," the captain goes on, "there are a lot of people out there"—she waves an arm, indicating the entire galaxy, I guess—"who don't want to be constantly watched and controlled by the StarLeague." She shoots a quick glance at Electra. "They don't like it when their children are taken and turned into soldiers, for example. For a long time this ship has delivered supplies to those who are trying to live outside the control of the StarLeague. Sometimes this means we get into places and deal with people who are dangerous. And let's say that sometimes . . . well . . . sometimes we . . ."

"You get into trouble," I say. I think I know where this is going. "You *like* trouble."

"Heh. Yes." The captain pulls out a chair from the table and sits down, folding her arms. "It occurred to me," she goes on, "when the Hunter appeared on this ship, that in certain situations it might be a very useful—"

"—weapon," I interrupt. "That's why you let me stay?"

She shakes her head, *no*. "I wouldn't want the Hunter if it didn't come with Trouble. Everyone else on this ship feels the same way." Then she gives her mysterious half smile. "What do you say—both of you. Will you join my crew?"

Electra and I look at each other. "I will if you will," I tell her.

"Yes," Electra answers, with a nod for the captain. "I don't want to be the StarLeague's weapon anymore."

"Good," I say. "I'll come too if we can go rescue the shapeshifters."

"Fine," Captain Astra says. "Yes. I don't like it, but we'll do it." She sits up and points at us. "I'll tell you this much. We're all in this together. And we're not doing anything until we have a plan. A very carefully thought-out, well-considered, intelligent plan in which neither of you children does anything stupid that requires us to rescue you."

Electra and I look at each other. We're both thinking, *Us? Children?*

"All right?" the captain asks.

"All right," we say at the same time.

39

When we start working on the plan, we real-ize pretty quickly that the only way to get into the StarLeague weapons lab aboard the *Peacemaker* is for me to do it. Anybody else in the crew would be detected immediately, because they all have ID chips and I don't.

Electra and I are studying the schematic—an incredibly detailed 3D map version of General Smag's ship made of blue lines and numbers. It's almost like the *Peacemaker* itself is floating in the screen on the wall.

"This is what I was talking about," the captain complains from the galley, where she's making yet another cup of kaff. "It's a stupid plan, and it puts Trouble in too much danger."

Electra ignores her. "You could go in through the waste disposal system, here," she says, pointing to a place in the schematic.

"What if I go in," I suggest, "and disable the ID chip detectors, and then you could come in here?" I point to another place, where I think the lab is located.

Electra studies it. Her tintacles turn red—a thinking color. "Hm. Maybe."

Leaving the galley, the captain crosses the room to flop onto the couch. "Trouble's going to get hurt, I just know it. I hate this."

"Yes," Electra says without looking at her. "We know."

Electra and I study the schematic for a while in silence.

"We're going about this the wrong way," she says at last.

"Yep," I agree.

"As soon as you shift, you'll give off that energy signal and the *Peacemaker* will know exactly where you are," Electra points out.

"I know." It's clear that sneaking in is not going to work.

Electra's eyes brighten, and for the very first time, she smiles—a wide, conspiratorial grin—and her tintacles turn bright green. "What about brave Cadet Electra Zox and—"

"—and her shapeshifter prisoner?" I finish, with an answering grin.

"Captain Astra is going to hate it," she says.

"I'm going to hate what?" the captain calls from the couch. She appears to be so relaxed that she has no bones, but I know her better than that. She's paying keen attention.

Electra turns from the table to face her. "We can't sneak in. The *Peacemaker* is too well defended."

I feel a sparkle of excitement. "So we take the Dart and fly it to Smag's ship. We pretend that Electra captured me, and walk right in."

"*What?*" the captain says, and leaps up from the couch. "That's a terrible idea." She strides over to the screen, where she examines the schematic. She points. "What if Trouble shifted into something small and went in through the—"

"Quit poking your nose in," Electra says crossly. "We already thought of that, and it won't work."

"What about—" the captain begins.

Electra interrupts her again. "Here's how you can help, Captain. If Trouble and I do manage to free the shapeshifters from the lab, you can figure out what we're going to do next." She holds up one finger. "First, as I've been telling you all along, General Smag is relentless. The stealth-box can't hide us forever. How are we going to get away from his pursuit?" She holds up a second finger. "Then, speaking of *we*, officially, I am still a StarLeague cadet, and if I'm really going to be a member of your crew, we'll have to do something about that. And three"—a third finger—"what about Trouble?"

"And the other shapeshifters," I put in. "The StarLeague thinks we're weapons. How can we make them see that we're people, too?"

"Oh, sure," the captain mutters. "Give me the hardest job—figuring out the aftermath." She stalks back over to the couch, flings herself down, puts her feet up, and closes her eyes.

Electra and I go back to the schematic of the weapons lab. The eye comes and hovers at my shoulder, watching. I tell Electra that The Knowledge asked me to look for information about it.

"Was it created in this weapons lab too?" Electra asks.

"Maybe," I tell her. "It will find out while we're there."

There's quiet for a few minutes while Electra and I study the schematic.

"I just thought of an even better way," I say, "for us to get into the lab. And I won't even have to shapeshift."

I tell her.

Electra's eyes gleam. "T, that is *devious*!"

"It is," I say proudly. "All we need is a rat."

Quietly, Electra and I add to our plan, discussing where in the lab the shapeshifters might be imprisoned, and figuring out what we're going to do about my missing ID chip.

Then, from the couch, the captain says, "Heh."

"What?" Electra asks, looking over at her.

Lying there with her eyes closed, the captain gives a broad, lazy smile. "We're going to get out of this just fine. And The Knowledge is going to help us do it."

40

We already know that General Smag is hunting for the *Hindsight*.

So it's not hard for *us* to hunt for *him*.

All we have to do is wait, hidden in our space-pocket.

The Knowledge's asteroid is nearby, and it keeps sending us snippets of advice and information, which we mostly have to ignore because we have a lot to do in the hour before *Peacemaker* arrives.

The whole crew helps.

While two Shkkka examine the schematic of General Smag's ship to see if there's anything we missed, Telly stations himself in the galley.

"Stew," he says, handing me a full bowl and a spoon, "with meat in it." Before I'm finished eating, he comes back and hands me a couple of protein bars. Then he brings a pile of lettuce from the garden. "Salad," he says with a tusky smile and a twitch of his ear that makes his bell earring tinkle. I eat the salad, and everything else that he brings me so that I can store up plenty of energy. Reetha works on Electra's old ID scanner so we can use it to get on board the *Peacemaker*, and one of the Shkkka prepares the Dart ship. Amby helps me find a rat who is willing to help us. The captain insists there are no rats on her ship, but of course there are. As it happens, the rats are eager to colonize *Peacemaker*, so they select a female pregnant with nine babies to come with us. She knows that it will be dangerous, but that's rats for you: they'll risk anything to expand their territory.

Electra puts on her black StarLeague coverall, and gives me a spare one she had in the Dart to put on. Using a sharp knife from the galley, Reetha gives me a short military haircut. While I eat protein bars, Electra drills me on how to stand and how to salute and even how to walk like a StarLeague cadet. The cadets are supposed to all do everything the exact same way, like proper little weapons. Electra says, with a frustrated growl, that I will never make a good cadet because I am very good at being Trouble, and not good at pretending to be somebody else.

When she says this, it makes the captain laugh for some reason.

Before we get into the Dart to leave on our mission, the rest of the crew comes to the cargo hold to wish us *good luck*, which is a thing people do, even though it doesn't have any effect on what happens.

Lizardians do not hug; Reetha just points a claw at me and says, "Come. Back."

I can't promise that we will, so I just nod.

Telly puts a big hand on my shoulder, and on Electra's. He smiles around his tusks. "Teach that Smag to leave us alone."

Beside him, Amby is crying. Fat blue tears run down their face. They wipe at them with long fingers. "I don't . . ." They sniff. "Please be . . ."

Then all three Shkkka surround Electra and me and pat us on our heads with their antennae.

Right before we get into the Dart, Captain Astra gives me a hug. When she does, I get that warm, safe feeling. "Be careful," she says.

"We will be," I assure her.

"No, we won't," Electra puts in. She climbs into the Dart and starts punching buttons on the control panel. The Knowledge's eye hovers at her shoulder, watching.

"Listen, Trouble," the captain says before I can follow. And then, in a quiet, serious voice, she tells me something big and important, and gives me another hug. "Good luck, you impossible creature," she says.

"Come *on*, T!" Electra shouts.

I pick up the rat in her cage.

Once I'm on the Dart, Electra takes us out of the hidden

Hindsight, setting a course that will lead us to *Peacemaker*.

Captain Astra will take the *Hindsight* and go to the far side of the Vault planet, staying dark and unnoticed but ready to swoop in to pick us up and then run for it if we have to.

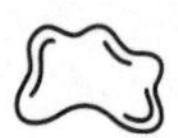

It isn't long before *Peacemaker* arrives.

At first I don't see it. I'm not expecting something that huge. As it moves it's just a shadow blotting out the stars. Then it turns and catches the light from the distant sun. The light flickers along the *Peacemaker*'s edges, and we see its sleek, dangerous lines and its powerful weapons. Lined up along its belly are Dart ships just like this one, tiny against the huge bulk of the ship.

We get closer, and *Peacemaker* fills the entire forward window.

Electra is communicating with it, giving the right codes in a flat, steady voice, but not telling them anything about the shapeshifter she has with her. She brings the Dart closer, then slots it into a row of other Darts. It lands with a loud, metallic clank and a shudder, and clamps come out and lock us into place.

I am so full of energy and nervousness and excitement that I can hardly keep my human skin on. This is my plan. I have to rescue the shapeshifters. I don't know what I'm going to do if it doesn't work.

"Relax," Electra says without looking away from the control panel. "Just be normal."

Yes, but the next part is the trickiest. Our entire mission could end right here.

We go to the outer hatch of the Dart, and Electra takes a deep breath. "Here we go," she tells me, and then hits the button to open it, and we step, in unison, onto the *Peacemaker*. The Knowledge's eye sneaks out behind us and then zips off to watch from farther away—but it's still recording everything that it sees.

We're at the *Peacemaker*'s dock, where all its Dart ships come in. It's a big, gleaming space, with rows of bright lights along a high ceiling, and various busy beings wearing military uniforms or black coveralls like the ones Electra and I have on.

As our feet hit the metal deck, two young cadets in coveralls bustle up to us, one long-necked lizardian and one humanoid whose face is covered with folds and wrinkles of pink skin. Their beady pink eyes peer out suspiciously at us.

"Report!" the humanoid orders.

Beside me, Electra stiffens and becomes the same Electra who first set foot on the *Hindsight*. "Senior Cadet Pilot Electra Zox," she snaps, then nods at me. "With Junior Cadet Trouble Hindsight." Briskly, she pulls from her coverall pocket her ID scanner, which Reetha fixed up for us. Electra scans her own ID and holds the device out for the other cadets to see. They nod, and she holds the device to my neck and secretly pushes another button that makes a fake ID come up: *Trouble Hindsight, human, junior cadet in the StarLeague military.* She shows it to the cadets, and they nod again. So far, so good.

Now for the tricky part.

"As ordered by General Smag," Electra says, "I have, with this cadet's assistance, captured the escaped shapeshifter." She points at the cage that I'm holding.

"That is a rat," says the wrinkled pink humanoid dubiously, peering at it.

"It is *not*," Electra says scornfully. "It is a shapeshifter that has taken a rat form." On cue, the rat hisses and bites at the mesh of its cage, its scaly tail thrashing and its whiskers bristling.

The humanoid takes half a step back, frightened. "Won't it escape?"

"No," Electra says in a *don't be stupid* voice. "The cage is made of a special top-secret material that prevents the shape-shifter from shifting. It is not a danger to you." Then she lowers her voice to a menacing whisper. "Unless the door to the cage somehow were to open. Then it would shift into a monster beyond your wildest fears and destroy you and everyone else on this ship."

As she speaks to the trembling cadets, I catch a glimpse, on the other side of the dock, of an officer in a StarLeague military uniform, along with four soldiers, marching in our direction.

Electra sees them too, but she doesn't get flustered. Still speaking briskly, like somebody used to giving orders and being obeyed, she says, "Now Cadet Hindsight will take the shape-shifter to your commanding officer." And then, without allowing the cadets to say another word, she spins on her heel and marches back toward her Dart.

Leaving me on the dock with a rat in a cage.

41

Electra wasn't happy with this part of the plan, and neither was the captain, but in the end they agreed that it made sense. While Electra waits in the Dart, I'm supposed to get to the lab where the shapeshifters are imprisoned. Once I've rescued them, I get them back to the Dart, we fly to the *Hindsight*, and escape. Simple, right?

What I wasn't expecting to see is General Smag marching toward us, followed by a bunch of StarLeague soldiers.

Seeing Smag's bulging forehead and jutting chin gives me a jolt of fright, but I stick to the plan.

"Ow!" I shout, and drop the rat's cage. "It bit me!"

As the cage hits the metal deck, its door pops open and the rat bursts out.

The pink humanoid cadet shrieks and jumps back, bumping

into the lizardian cadet; they both stumble aside, colliding with two of the approaching soldiers. The rat darts through the tangle of legs, scurrying for the nearest shadowy hiding place.

Go, rat, go!

"The shapeshifter!" I shout. "It has escaped!" I point in a random direction. "Quick! Chase it!"

Somehow my shouts don't have the same effect as Electra's orders.

Instead of going after the rat, General Smag has stopped; his soldiers have their weapons drawn, protecting him. He is already issuing commands.

"You"—he points at the wrinkly pink cadet—"report to the energy-tracking crew; alert them that the shapeshifter is on the ship. And you"—he points at the lizardian—"report to the lab and tell them to lock down and raise the threat level."

Then he turns his piercing black eyes on me. "You"—he points at me, and my heart freezes in my chest, even though I know he's never seen me in my human form—"you're with me, Cadet." With that, he turns on his heel and strides across the deck, barking more orders as he goes.

Surrounded by soldiers, I follow him off the dock, into a corridor, and then through a wide door into what must be the *Peacemaker*'s bridge—its control center. It is a vast room with a gleaming metallic floor; there are ranks of control panels, blinking with buttons and schematics and flashing lights. In the middle of the bridge is the command chair. Rushing around are more soldiers and young cadets, and some nervous-looking people in white lab coats—scientists. The general strides onto the bridge, followed by his bodyguards. I try to slither off at the last second, but one of the soldiers reaches back and drags me in with them.

"Close the doors," the general orders. "Initiate emergency external-protection protocols."

A soldier punches a button on a control panel, and a light starts to flash red, and a heavy metal wall studded with rivets slides down from the ceiling and locks into place over the bridge's door.

This isn't part of the plan. I'm supposed to be pretending to chase the rat while heading for the lab deep inside the *Peacemaker*. I have to free the shapeshifters!

Instead I'm trapped in a room with fifty soldiers and General Smag.

A blink, and I could shift into the Hunter and fight my way out.

But no. Not yet. The most important part of our plan is that nobody gets hurt, not if we can help it.

One of the soldiers nearby casts me a frowning look, and I realize that I don't look very cadet-like. Quickly, I go to the edge of the room, where I stand stiffly, the way Electra taught me.

The Knowledge's eye, I realize, is hovering at my shoulder.

"Shhh," I whisper to it. "Stay hidden."

Another soldier glances over at me; her antennae twitch

suspiciously. I snap to attention again, staring straight ahead. The room is noisy with soldiers at the control panels, talking on communication devices, reporting to other soldiers.

"Sensors!" General Smag orders. He is standing at a control panel, looming over the shoulder of a junior officer. "Has it shifted yet?"

"No energy spike, sir," the officer reports.

"It's still in the rat form, then," the general says. He knows that I give off that rare energy when I shift from one shape to another. "Continue to monitor. It must be captured."

That's when he decides he's ready to question the junior cadet who brought in the shapeshifter.

"You," he snaps, whirling around to face me. He points. "Report."

"Me?" I blurt out.

General Smag's all-black beady eyes stare at me as he comes closer, flanked by two of his bodyguards. His heavy footsteps ring on the metal deck. My human boy shape was new to me when I went onto the *Hindsight*, so he's never seen me as Trouble. Still, all I can think as he comes closer is that he can *see* me, he *has* to!

"You captured the shapeshifter," he says in his deep, commanding voice. "How?"

"It . . ." I stammer. I am not good at this. "It was in its rat form, and we caught it in the cage."

"We?" the general prompts.

"Me and Electra," I explain. "She's—the other cadet. The Dart pilot." I step away until my back is against the metal wall, but still the general leans in, examining me. "The rat went right into the cage."

His eyes narrow with suspicion. "You are speaking of the most powerful being in the galaxy."

Really?

"And it went into the cage without a fight?" he asks.

"Yep," I say. "Just walked right in."

"If it allowed itself to be captured so easily . . ." The general straightens and turns away. "It intended to come here." He snaps out another order. "Prepare for an attack."

"Sir," puts in a soldier; her frondy antennae twitch. "Surely we are safe on the bridge. The shapeshifter cannot get in here?"

I almost laugh. They're not as safe as they think they are.

Somehow the general senses this; he swings back around. "You think this is funny, Cadet?"

"Well," I admit. "A little."

The general stalks back toward me. His beady eyes glare. "You're no StarLeague cadet," he realizes. He looms over me, threatening. "Who *are* you?"

In response, the Hunter stirs inside me. "I'm Trouble," I tell him.

A vein in his bulgy forehead pulses. "Trouble? What do you mean, trouble?"

"General!" calls the junior officer, who is gaping at a readout on the control panel. “We’re seeing a buildup in the shapeshifter energy signal. It’s preparing to shift.” The officer’s voice grows higher with alarm. “Sir, the signal is coming from *here*. The shapeshifter is here! It is inside this room— It is right . . .” She turns, searching, and then points at me.

“. . . there!”

42

General Smag straightens—tall and broad, he stares down at me. "*You.*"

"Me," I say, and give him my best smile.

He backs away; the rest of the soldiers are pulling out their weapons, but half of them look confused—they haven't figured out that the innocent-seeming cadet Trouble is a lot more devious than he looks.

"The rat was a decoy," the general concludes. "The senior cadet. Electra Zox. She has betrayed her orders. Scan for her ID chip," he says over his shoulder. "Is she on the station?"

She shouldn't be. She should be safely on the Dart, waiting to pick me up after I rescue the shapeshifters.

"Yes, sir," answers a soldier at a control panel.

Oh no. Electra didn't follow the plan—she didn't go back

onto the Dart, as she was supposed to. She must have seen that I got picked up by General Smag. Knowing Electra, she's gone to rescue the shapeshifters herself.

The general's big chin juts. "Track her," he orders his soldiers. And they can, because Electra has an ID chip that shows them exactly where she is on the *Peacemaker*.

"We've got her, sir," the officer at the control panel says in a shaking voice while glancing nervously at me. "She's in a corridor outside the weapons lab." He pauses, listening. "Sir, the lab is locked down—she is trapped there."

"Send soldiers after her!" General Smag orders. The officer obeys, barking the command into a communication device. "Tell them to shoot to kill."

"No!" I shout. "Leave her alone!"

As my voice rings out, the soldiers bring their weapons to bear on me. One of them loses their battle with fright and pulls the trigger—

—but it's too late, because I have already shifted.

Distantly, my Hunter ears hear screaming and shouted orders echoing across the *Peacemaker*'s bridge, but I pay little attention to them, or to the energy bolts whanging off my armored skin.

Electra. The Hunter must get to Electra before General

Smag's shoot-to-kill order is carried out. Then—rescue the other shapeshifters.

I spend a nanosecond studying the reinforced door, analyzing it for weaknesses. There are none. Still, I run at the door, ramming a shoulder into a riveted seam. There is an echoing clang, but the door is barely dented.

General Smag, the Hunter realizes, is still shouting orders into a communication device.

The soldiers scream and shout and scatter as I whirl, leap over a bank of control panels, landing with a heavy thump on my clawed feet. The general stumbles back while another soldier scrambles under a nearby chair as I bring a claw down, shattering the controls at the communication station. I spit a ball of concentrated acid onto another panel and it starts to disintegrate, the air filling with the acrid smell of melted plastic.

Electra. She's in trouble *right now*. The Hunter must save her.

I leap onto the control panels and then hurl my entire heavy weight at the metal door and again it dents—but holds.

Electra! I roar.

And then, strangely, everything around the Hunter slows down. I see General Smag ducking to hide behind the command chair; I smell the smoke rising up from the smashed panels; I see The Knowledge's shiny metal eye hovering just below the ceiling; I see a humanoid soldier pointing a weapon and closing her eyes as she fires it, and I hear the sizzle of the energy bolt burning through the air as it travels toward me and I reach out and brush it aside. I turn back to the wall and realize that everything around me seems slow because the Hunter is moving extremely fast.

I have shifted—but not my shape. I have shifted into the gaps between seconds.

Huh, as the captain would say. I didn't know I could do this!

The Hunter turns and studies the door again. It shimmers as if it is a silver curtain. To the Hunter, the wall is only a small thing that is in its way. Again I rush toward it, only this time my shoulder doesn't crash into it, denting the metal. Instead I shift between each molecule of the wall, as easily as stepping through a doorway. A flash, and I'm out the other side, into a corridor where a troop of soldiers is really wonderfully surprised to see me.

"The shapeshifter!" one of them screams.

Here comes Trouble! I roar back at them, and they fling themselves out of my way as I start down the corridor, heading for the lab, where Electra is trapped.

43

Outside the ship's bridge, all is chaos and red lights and infrared lights flashing and energy bolts zipping past and soldiers shouting, and what looks like General Smag and a bunch of his bodyguards hurrying down another corridor—but I ignore all of it, heading for the passageway that leads to the lab, where Electra is in trouble. It's a straight, narrow corridor with lights along the edges of the ceiling. As I lope down it, the lights go out—but the Hunter, I find, can see in the dark. I catch sight of the end of the corridor, but before I reach it, an emergency door irises shut—a blast door, part of their emergency lockdown. I do my new phase-shift thing and pass right through it.

Strangely, when I stride through the closed door, The Knowledge's eye is waiting for me on the other side—watching everything.

I race into another corridor, and from around a corner I hear the sound of weapons firing and the shout of orders. I race in that direction. As I pass, I see that in the outside walls of the corridor are recessed doors—the entryways into the weapons lab in the science area. Thanks to the schematic that The Knowledge gave us, I know exactly where I am, and where I have to go.

As I come closer, I see the backs of StarLeague uniforms and the flash of energy bolts. They're huddled behind a corner, popping out to fire at one of the recessed doors. From that cave-like space comes the flash of weapons fire.

Electra. She's there, trapped.

I lope up behind the StarLeague soldiers.

Excuse me.

At the sound of my claws on the deck, one of them, an insectoid, looks over her carapaced shoulder. Seeing me, she screeches and drops her weapon. The rest of them whirl, and a few fire their weapons, the energy bolts deflecting off me. One bolt ricochets from a wall and almost hits another soldier, except that I reach out and catch it with my claw. With my other claw I grab a few weapons and crush them. A roar from me, and all five of the soldiers take off running, screaming as they go.

As they flee, I take three bounding steps and reach the door where Electra is hiding.

She has her back propped against the wall and an array of weapons lined up on the floor next to her.

Her face is keen and resolute, her tintacles are bright blue, and she has a smear of red across her chin.

Red. *Blood.*

She is injured.

"Hello, Trouble," she gasps, and starts trying to climb to her feet.

I shift into my human form. "How badly are you hurt?" I ask.

She grabs the wall to steady herself. "Not bad." She gasps again as she tries to put weight on one leg. "But not good, either."

"I'll get you back to your Dart," I tell her, and before she can argue, I shift into my Hunter form and swing her into my arms. In this shape I'm not a lot bigger than my human boy form, but I am much, *much* stronger.

"Ow!" she protests, wriggling.

Spikes on my shoulders. *Sorry!* Trying not to drip any acid from my fangs on her, I start back toward the corridor that leads away from the science area. Halfway down it, we reach the emergency door that I phase-shifted through—which I can't do with Electra in my arms.

"Wait!" she calls, and points to the panel next to the door. "I know the protocols." She pauses to catch her breath. "And the codes." I take her closer and she leans over and hits a few buttons, and the door dilates open, and I hurry through it and keep going until I reach the dock.

On the dock, which I passed through on my way to find

Electra, are scorch marks from energy bolts and a few discarded weapons, and the red and infrared lights are still flashing, and an emergency warning appears on all the screens, but there's not a single StarLeague soldier. With my claws skidding on the shiny floor, I hurry to the Dart, where I set Electra carefully down and shift into my human shape again.

"Come on," she says, gripping the frame of the outer hatch with bloody fingers.

"No," I tell her. "You go. I still have to rescue the shape-shifters."

"Trouble," she growls. "There is no way. You can't even get in there—believe me, I tried."

"The Hunter can get in," I tell her, and I don't mention that I'm not sure I can get out again. "But I have to hurry. If too many of those StarLeague soldiers join the fight, somebody will end up getting hurt."

"Weapon," she says, and gives me a bleak smile.

"Weapon yourself," I say, and pat her on the shoulder. "Go back to the *Hindsight*. Ask the captain to please pick up me and the shifters outside *Peacemaker*. Tell her to hurry, because I'll be in my blob of goo form, and I don't want to forget her or you or anybody. All right?"

She gives me a brisk nod.

I give her a nod back. "Electra," I ask, "what emotion are you feeling when your tintacles are orange?"

She reaches up and pulls a tintacle down so she can see it.

"Worry," she answers. Then she goes on. "Worry that a person I care about is going to get hurt."

"Me?" I ask. "You're worried about me?"

"Of course I am," she snaps. She lets the tintacle go, and it waves at me. "Just be careful, all right?"

Before I can inform her that I'm the most powerful person in the galaxy—General Smag said so!—she turns and hobbles onto the Dart, the outer hatch closing behind her. Before we set out, Shkkka had rigged the Dart to disconnect from the *Peacemaker*'s clamps. Electra will be fine, and she'll get safely to the *Hindsight* and deliver my message to the captain.

And now I can do what I came here to do. I shift.

I am the Hunter, and nobody and nothing can stop me now.

44

The Hunter is in a hurry.

I race down the deserted corridor toward the science area—and the high-security weapons lab. It looks like the StarLeague has figured out that attacking me doesn't do them much good. Followed by The Knowledge's eye, I phase-shift through a door and step into the lab.

Once there, I shift into my human form because I want to see it through my human boy eyes, to see if it's like the bad dream that I had when I was in The Knowledge's Vault.

The weapons lab is an empty white space and not very big. It's just a room. It's quiet. So quiet, it feels like my ears are listening for something that should be there but isn't. Against the inner wall are machines and metal plates and a long countertop. Above them are screens that are blank. There's a doorway; I go through it into a similar room—another lab—and then another.

None of it is familiar, and there's no trace of any other shapeshifters.

The air is cold, so I pause and take a white lab coat from a hook and put it on, rolling up the sleeves as I go through another door into yet another lab. My bare feet make no sound on the metal floor.

I pause. The same white walls, the same cold machinery, the same blank screen . . . and yet it feels familiar.

For some reason little bumps are crawling over my skin, making me shiver.

I have been here before.

For just a flash I get a piece of the bad dream. Me in another form—something with a lot of legs and eyes, something that felt fear and pain very keenly.

Then—a needle. It injected me with cells from another organism—and I was forced to take that shape. And then another shape and another, and through it all I tried as hard as I could to remain myself, holding on to who I am—to *me*.

Fighting. Resisting. Trying to escape, and failing, over and over again.

Always alone.

Another flash, and I'm back, shivering in the lab, the floor icy cold under my bare feet.

I couldn't have been alone through all of that, could I? There were other shapeshifters. Weren't there?

“I knew I would find you here,” comes a deep voice from behind me.

I whirl. It is General Smag. He came so silently through the door and into the lab that I didn’t hear him. Behind him, two of his bodyguards file into the room, wearing black uniforms, their weapons drawn. More soldiers wait outside.

I tense, ready to shift back into the Hunter.

The general raises a broad hand, and his bodyguards lower their weapons. He steps closer. “You came here to destroy the lab. Is that correct?”

I study him carefully. He doesn’t seem afraid.

Well, Trouble isn’t that scary.

And he must be getting continual reports on what I’ve been doing—and he knows that not a single one of his soldiers or cadets has been hurt by the Hunter.

I back away, wary. “No,” I say finally. “I came to save the other shapeshifters.”

His broad face doesn’t react to that, but somehow he seems surprised. Then he holds up both of his hands. It’s a thing humanoids do, to show that they are not holding a weapon—that they are harmless.

General Smag is not harmless, but I nod.

“Come,” he says in his commanding voice. “I will show you the . . . other shapeshifters.” He points to the door leading to the next room.

Ready, in case it’s a trap, I back away from him and then

edge through the door; he follows. His bodyguards, smooth and deadly, take their positions behind him. General Smag crosses the lab to a counter. There is a clear box on it. The box is empty. Or . . . no. In the box is . . .

I squint my human eyes to see better. Is it a . . . ?

General Smag picks up the box, brings it to a metal table in the middle of the room, and roughly turns it over.

A blob of goo oozes out of it, then spreads across the tabletop. It looks like a clear, round, slightly shiny puddle.

"Is that a shapeshifter?" I ask, because it looks a little like me in my blob of goo form.

"It is nothing," the general answers. He pokes the goo with a broad finger. It makes an indentation. "Raw material," he goes on. "Shapeless. Nameless. An empty thing to be filled. We experimented with this other template, but it didn't work." He points at me. "You were the only success."

I take a shaky breath, realizing something. "You didn't just want to capture me because I'm the Hunter and I'm a weapon. You also want to know why I became a shapeshifter when you failed with that one." I point at the blob. Then I realize something else. "You didn't mean for me to become a person."

"You are not a person," the general says calmly. "You are a created monster that was made using bits and pieces of other creatures, other beings. There is no *you*."

"I am me," I tell him. "I am my own self. I am Trouble."

"No," Smag insists, absolutely sure of what he is saying.

"There is only the weapon—and even if the weapon escapes again from here, the StarLeague military will track it to the ends of the galaxy. It will be recaptured, the *Hindsight* will be destroyed, and its crew will go to prison."

Relentless, Electra called him. It's true.

I can only see two solutions to this problem.

One, the Hunter kills General Smag, and kills or injures a whole lot of people on the *Peacemaker*, and blasts out of here.

The Hunter is a weapon. But even though I was made for hunting and killing, I get to decide what I really am. I am not going to kill General Smag, or anybody else.

There's only one other thing I can do.

I hop up to sit on the table next to the puddle of blob and offer General Smag a deal that he'd never make if I really was a weapon. "What if I agree to let you recapture me now?"

The general is huge and looming; his black eyes glitter. He nods. "That would serve my purpose," he says. "You will remain here, in the lab, so that our weapons specialists can study you and replicate their success in creating the shapeshifter as a weapon."

A shiver runs through me. I think he's saying that they want to take me apart to figure out how I work. But I am what I am: a person who will let the general take me apart if it means saving the people I love.

"You'll have to let them go if I stay here," I say. "Captain Astra and the rest. And Electra, too."

"They will not be charged with a crime for hiding you from the StarLeague," he says. Four of his bodyguards have lined up behind him; they have their weapons trained on me.

With a tip of my finger, I touch the surface of the blob of goo spread over the table. It feels warm. I look up at Smag. "That's not enough," I tell him. "You have to let them go free, completely."

Smag's beady black eyes are fixed on me. "Very well. The weapon stays here, in the lab, and the *Hindsight* and its crew go free. Agreed?"

"Yes," I say, feeling a pit full of frozen misery water open up inside me. Strangely, the puddle of goo responds by turning suddenly cold. "I agree."

And then The Knowledge's eye drops down from where it was hovering near the ceiling and goes completely haywire.

45

The eye makes a high-pitched squealing noise. Slowly, it starts to spin; it picks up speed until it is whirling around and around, flinging off sparks and sprouting antennae like silvery spines.

General Smag stares at it, his all-black eyes narrowed. He'd been so busy with me that he hadn't even noticed the eye lurking near the ceiling.

His bodyguards tense, and other soldiers pile into the room, weapons drawn.

I stay where I am, sitting on the table next to the blob of goo.

The eye emits another high shriek and slowly spins to a halt.

Then, vibrating from every surface in the lab, the deep, echoing voice of The Knowledge rings out.

All people in every part of the galaxy, it says, *are seeing this broadcast. All are seeing what you are about to see and hearing what you can hear.*

And then all the screens in the lab flicker to brilliant, colorful life. All the screens on *Peacemaker* are showing this—no, every screen on every station and every ship and every planet in the entire galaxy, broadcast by The Knowledge.

A series of images flash across the screen. Captain Astra with me in the galley, drinking kaff and talking. Me handing Shkkka tools while she works on the Dart. Telly showing me a flower that bloomed on one of his plants. Reetha trying to teach me to be a better player of the strategy game. Me and Amby carefully becoming friends again. Electra showing me how to stand like a cadet, and scolding me for laughing. Electra, who was taken from her family and never got to be a kid. And always the ship, *Hindsight*, with its warmth and color and safety. Home.

Then the images slow down, and change. Now the screens all over the galaxy show The Knowledge's room on the asteroid, the moment when my captain stepped out of the wall made of light, crossed the room, and stopped to open her arms. Then it shows human boy Trouble running to her, and the captain enfolding him in a hug. Kissing the top of his head.

You're all right? the captain on the screen asks.

Yes, Trouble answers. *Are* you *all right?*

From here I can see what I couldn't see when the captain was hugging me. Her face is full of worry and fear—and then it smooths out. *I am now*, I hear her say.

Then the screens shift again. Now they show this place—the weapons lab five minutes ago, as The Knowledge's eye saw it. On the screen a hulking General Smag stands on one side of a table with a puddle of goo on it. Sitting on the table is much smaller Trouble wearing a white lab coat.

You'll have to let them go if I stay here, Trouble says. *Captain Astra and the rest. And Electra too.*

They will not be charged with a crime for hiding you from the StarLeague, General Smag answers.

On the screen, Trouble touches a finger to the puddle of goo, and it shimmers in the bright lights of the lab.

That's not enough, Trouble says. *You'll have to let them go free, completely.*

Very well, General Smag says, up there on the screen. *The weapon stays here in the lab, and the* Hindsight *and its crew go free. Agreed?*

On the screen, the Trouble sitting on the table looks down at the puddle of goo. *Yes,* he says, and his voice sounds quiet and sad. *I agree.*

I realize that the captain has been watching all along on the *Hindsight.*

She's probably not very happy with me right now.

But then my captain's dry, drawling voice, broadcast by The Knowledge's eye, booms out, echoing through the lab and, I guess, through every ship and station and planet in the entire galaxy:

Hello there, General Smag. Captain Astra of the Hindsight *here. Maybe you have forgotten that according to the laws of the StarLeague, a being is considered a person when it is self-aware and conscious and has an identity. Whether somebody is a person is not determined by their gender identity or place of origin or species.*

It does not matter that Trouble was raised in a StarLeague lab, created to be a weapon. What he is, *without any doubt, and according to the laws of the StarLeague, is a person. The scenes you just saw prove it. As a person, Trouble has certain rights and a claim on galactic citizenship, and he cannot be imprisoned against his will if he has not been convicted of a crime.*

Ohhh. My captain *planned* all of this—with The Knowledge. *This* is how she figured out how to deal with the aftermath.

Silly Trouble, I tell myself. You forgot that the captain is way more devious than you are.

Captain Astra is still speaking. She says something about how I wasn't issued an ID chip when I was born, which means the StarLeague has broken its own laws, and she says that the StarLeague has no authority to separate a child from its family and that I must be returned at once to the *Hindsight*, blah blah blah.

General Smag is listening to this with his mouth pinched in fury and his eyes glittering and a vein on his forehead pulsing and his big hands clenched at his sides. But there's nothing he can do. The entire galaxy knows that he's done something wrong. He's beaten and he knows it—by his own laws! His soldiers are staring at the screens with their mouths open, their weapons drooping at their sides.

I'm not paying much attention to any of it.

Because I am looking down at the puddle of goo on the table next to me. It was warm when I first touched it, and then it went cold when I felt the most sad and alone. It glimmers in the lights of the lab. As I look at it, the tiniest pseudopod extends from its surface. When I reach out to it, the pseudopod wraps around the tip of my finger and holds on.

"Don't worry, little shifter," I whisper to it. "I'm getting out of here. And when I go, I'm not going to leave you behind."

46

Captain Astra has stopped speaking and the screens have gone dim again. The lab echoes with silence. The soldiers are still standing around, looking shocked. Then relentless General Smag decides to do something very stupid.

He pulls a weapon from his belt, aims it at The Knowledge's eye—

—and fires.

The energy bolt slams into the eye, which explodes like a tiny supernova in the middle of the lab.

At the same moment, General Smag starts shouting orders—something about *shapeshifter containment protocols*—and his bodyguards go on full alert, weapons out. An alarm blares and lights flash.

I shift into my Hunter form.

One of the guards charges at me. I blur out of her way, and she slams face-first into a wall. Ignoring the shouting and the energy bolts whizzing past me, I scoop the puddle of goo into its clear box, protecting it in the crook of my arm.

I pause to examine the shards of the eye, scattered over the floor. I feel a pang of sadness—poor little eye!—but I know The Knowledge will be all right, even without it. I have the strongest feeling that it found what it was looking for. The Knowledge must have suspected that it was created in a lab a lot like this one. It's like me—and that means it will keep thinking of ways to operate outside the control of the StarLeague. It is devious, after all.

I've realized, of course, that *devious* really means *very good at surviving.*

On my way out of the lab I see General Smag, who looks furious and has a weapon in each big hand. I wave at him. *Byeeee!*

He responds by shooting at me. I catch each bolt in my claw. He shoots again and I deflect the bolt so that it zings back toward him, sizzling right past his jutting jaw. He screams out something that sounds like a profanity.

General Smag.

Who is *relentless.*

The Hunter carefully sets the shapeshifter on the floor and then time-shifts. I dart from one soldier to the next, seizing each weapon, crumpling it, and dropping it to the floor. I don't like it when people shoot at each other.

When all the guards—and Smag—are disarmed, I shift back into my human form.

The soldiers gape at me. One of them reaches for a weapon in her belt that I missed.

"Don't even bother," I warn, and as the soldier raises her hands to show that she won't draw the weapon, I turn to face General Smag.

He is panting, and beads of black-tinted sweat are oozing from his bulgy forehead.

"You," I tell him, "will not bother me or the *Hindsight* or its crew or this baby shapeshifter ever again."

From where I'm standing I can hear his teeth grinding together.

"If you do," I go on, "the Hunter will come onto this ship and take it apart from the inside." I point at the room. "Starting from here." I step closer and lower my voice. "No more experiments. No more weapons."

Smag just glares at me.

Carefully, I raise one eyebrow. "Got it?"

"Yes," Smag grinds out. "Understood."

"Thank you," I say politely, and shift into the Hunter form.

As Smag and the soldiers watch, I pick up the shapeshifter in its box and head out the door. Quickly, I go through one empty lab, then another; then I race down a long, empty corridor—I remember from the schematics that there should be . . .

Ah, here. An airlock.

You remember how those work, right? The little room with an inner hatch door and an outer hatch door?

With a claw, I open the inner hatch and I step into the airlock, still carrying the shapeshifter blob.

I hit the button; as soon as the inner hatch door is closed, I pause to consider.

The *Hindsight* is coming, I know that much, but it may not be near enough. I can't risk shifting into my blob of goo form and forgetting everything.

The Hunter, after all, is the most powerful person in the galaxy. Surely *ebullism* isn't something I have to worry about.

So when I push the button for the outer hatch, I stay in my Hunter form, and when the outer hatch opens, the blob and I float peacefully away from the StarLeague's high-security weapons lab.

The *Peacemaker* departs.

And I am alone.

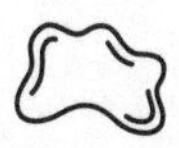

Space is big.

It's empty and black and cold, with faint, silent points of light that, when you get close to them, become stars seething with heat or busy stations or cloud-covered planets.

But mostly space is empty.

I remember what my captain once said to me. *People travel*

with you for a while, she said. *You're always alone in the end.*

But Captain Astra said something else to me too. The big, important thing that she told me when Electra and I were about to leave on our mission to rescue the shapeshifters.

I was wrong, she told me then. *Sometimes you don't end up alone. I will always come for you, Trouble*, she said. *Always.*

And Electra? I asked, because she and I needed to be kids together.

The captain smiled, and kissed the top of my head. *And your friend, yes.*

So I wait. And I think. And I listen.

There is no other person in the entire galaxy like the Hunter. It's made up of bits and pieces of other kinds of beings. It's a *mongrel*, just like my dog puppy form. Before, the Hunter was a monster. Now it's just me. I'm a kid. I'm a weapon for keeping the people I love safe. I'm waiting for my captain. She's coming; I know she is. And Reetha. And Shkkka and Telly and Amby. And Electra, my friend.

I wait and wait. Me and a blob of goo—who might, just might, be a baby shapeshifter.

The dark of space seems to go on forever.

And then, at last, a ship appears. It's a dented tin can of a ship, a lighter shadow against the darkness of space. As it comes closer, the outer hatch slides open. The Hunter gathers the blob and drifts nearer to it, then enters the airlock. The outer hatch slides closed. Air flows into the airlock. As it does, I shift.

The form I take is a completely familiar shape. A warm-blooded mammal. Soft body, no exoskeleton. Air breather. Hair on the top of my head. Hands, feet, face, a mouth for talking with.

A human.

When I open my human eyes, I can see the whole family waiting in the passage beyond the inner hatch. Reetha, Amby, Telly, all three Shkkka. Electra, with a bandage on her leg.

Captain Astra, who is smiling and crying at the same time.

I can't wait to tell her that while I was waiting for her to come for me, floating in the deep velvet of space, I heard it. I never thought I would, but I did.

I heard the sound of the stars, Captain.

They were singing.

Acknowledgments

Thanks to:

My besties: Deb Coates, Jenn Reese, and Greg van Eekhout.

My intrepid agent, Melanie Castillo, and everybody at Root Literary.

EditorK, the amazing Kelsey Murphy. Thanks also to the team at Philomel/Penguin Young Readers, including copyeditors Marinda Valenti and Abigail Powers, associate editor Cheryl Eissing, designer Monique Sterling, cover designer Tony Sahara, cover artist Pétur Antonsson, associate publisher Jill Santopolo, publisher Ken Wright, Elise Poston and Gerard Mancini in managing editorial, Kara Brammer in marketing, Lauren Festa in digital marketing, publicist Lizzie Goodell, Felicia Frazier and everyone in sales, Jocelyn Schmidt, and Jen Loja.

The Maud, John, and Pip, and all my dear families.

My wonderful colleagues at Prairie Lights Books in Iowa City.

For book help, Anna Catanese, Ali Borger-Germann, and Phillip Tyne.

Sukie Brown for the word *vegetably*.

And Taylor Swift, for the theme song.

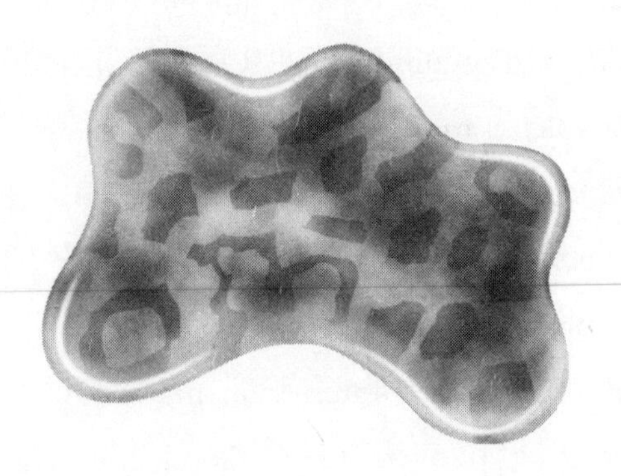